E.T Stevens, D Morris

Annotated Poems of English Authors

The Traveller, or, a Prospect of Society by Oliver Goldsmith

E.T Stevens, D Morris

Annotated Poems of English Authors
The Traveller, or, a Prospect of Society by Oliver Goldsmith

ISBN/EAN: 9783337212322

Printed in Europe, USA, Canada, Australia, Japan

Cover: Foto ©Andreas Hilbeck / pixelio.de

More available books at **www.hansebooks.com**

ANNOTATED POEMS
OF
ENGLISH AUTHORS

EDITED BY THE

REV. E. T. STEVENS, M.A. OXON.

Joint-Editor of 'The Grade Lesson-Books' 'The Useful Knowledge Series' &c.

AND THE

REV. D. MORRIS, B.A. LOND.

Author of 'The Class-Book History of England' &c.

THE TRAVELLER
OR, A PROSPECT OF SOCIETY
BY OLIVER GOLDSMITH

ADAM MILLER AND COMPANY

11 WELLINGTON STREET WEST

TORONTO

1878

OLIVER GOLDSMITH.

OLIVER GOLDSMITH, the son of an Irish clergyman, was born at Pallas, a very lonely village in county Longford, in the year 1728. He entered Trinity College, Dublin, at the age of seventeen, but his habits were so idle and extravagant that his college career was anything but satisfactory. His friends scarcely knew what to do with him, so reckless and careless had he become. At last he was sent to Edinburgh to study medicine, where he remained for two years, though with little profit to himself. He then went to study at Leyden for a year, and afterwards travelled on foot through France, Switzerland and Northern Italy, without money, and trusting only to his wits and his flute for support. In the year 1756 he landed at Dover, without a penny in his pocket or a friend to help him. At first he tried to get a living as a strolling player; then he became usher in a school for a short time; and, finally, he settled in London as an author. After a while he obtained the friendship of such great men as Dr. Johnson, Sir Joshua Reynolds the painter, Garrick the actor, and Edmund Burke the orator and statesman. In spite of his success, however, as a graceful writer, he was often in great difficulties through his reckless habits, and he eventually died in 1774, owing a large sum of money.

His chief prose works are his 'Chinese Letters,' afterwards published under the title of 'The Citizen of the World;' 'The Vicar of Wakefield;' the comedies of 'The Good-natured Man,' and 'She Stoops to Conquer;' the Histories of England, Rome, and Greece, and the 'History of Animated Nature,' which he left unfinished.

His chief poems are 'The Traveller,' 'The Deserted Village,' and 'The Hermit.' The first two poems will never be forgotten so long as the English language exists. 'The Traveller,' published in 1764, is a beautiful description of the social condition of the people of the different countries through which the author made his tour. Its aim is described in the Dedicatory Letter which the author addressed to his brother, the Rev. Henry Goldsmith. 'The Deserted Village' appeared in 1770. The aim of the author is described in the letter in which he dedicated the poem to his friend Sir Joshua Reynolds. He pictures an English village, with its pretty scenes and simple rural life, rendered desolate by falling into the possession of some wealthy merchant or tradesman; describes the hardships and miseries of the exiled peasantry; and ends by calling upon Poetry, as a goddess, to lessen or mitigate the evils he deplores. The various scenes and sketches of life in this poem are most beautiful and touching, and the musical cadence of its language most pleasing. It is, however, very faulty in design, for 'Sweet Auburn' is a picture of an English village, but in its desolate condition we have nothing but a ruined Irish hamlet, which the poet probably saw in his native island, but not in England.

The life of Oliver Goldsmith has been written by Mr. Prior, Mr. Washington Irving, and Mr. Forster; and of these Lord Macaulay says: 'The diligence of Mr. Prior deserves all praise; the style of Mr. Washington Irving is always pleasing; but the highest place must in justice be assigned to Mr. Forster.'

Garrick calls him 'Scholar, rake, Christian, dupe, gamester, and poet.' Dr. Johnson says: Oliver Goldsmith 'was a man of such variety of powers, and such felicity of performance, that he always seemed to do best that which he was doing ; a man who had the art of being minute without tediousness, and general without confusion ; whose language was copious without exuberance, exact without constraint, and easy without weakness. . . . Let not his frailties be remembered ; he was a very great man.'

Mr. Forster says : 'He worthily did the work that was in him to do ; proved himself in his garret a gentleman of nature : and left the world no ungenerous bequest.'

Sir Walter Scott says : 'The wreath of Goldsmith is unsullied : he wrote to exalt virtue and expose vice ; and he accomplished his task in the manner which raises him to the highest rank among British authors. We close his volume with a sigh that such an author should have written so little from the stores of his own genius, and that he should have been so prematurely removed from the sphere of literature which he adorned.'

CRITICISMS ON 'THE TRAVELLER.'

LORD MACAULAY says, 'In one respect "The Traveller" differs from all Goldsmith's other writings. In general, his designs were bad, and his execution good. In "The Traveller," the execution, though deserving of much praise, is far inferior to the design. No philosophical poem, ancient or modern, has a plan so noble, and at the same time so simple.' *Biographies.*

Mr. Forster says, 'Johnson pronounced it ("The Traveller,") a poem to which it would not be easy to find anything equal, since the death of Pope. Though covering but the space of twenty years, this was praise worth coveting, and was honestly deserved. The elaborate care and skill of the verse, the exquisite choice and selection of diction, at once recalled to others, as to Johnson, the master so lately absolute in the realms of verse; and with these, there was a rich harmony of tone, a softness and simplicity of touch, a happy and playful tenderness, which belonged peculiarly to the later poet. With a less pointed and practised force of understanding than in Pope, and in some respects less subtle and refined, the appeal to the heart in Goldsmith is more gentle, direct, and pure. The predominant impression of "The Traveller" is of its naturalness and facility; and there is felt the surpassing charm with which its everyday genial fancies invest high thoughts of human happiness. The serene graces of its style, and the mellow flow of its verse, take us captive, before we feel the enchantment of its lovely images of various life, reflected from its calm, still depths of philosophic contemplation. Above all, do we see that it is a poem built upon nature, that it rests upon honest truth, that it is not crying to the moon and stars for impossible sympathy, or dealing with other worlds, in fact or imagination, than the writer has himself lived in and known. Wisely had Goldsmith avoided what in the false-heroic versifiers of his day he had wittily condemned, the practice, even commoner since, of building up poetry on fantastic unreality, of clothing it in harsh inversions of language, and of patching it out with affectations of bygone vivacity, "as if the more it was unlike prose, the more it would resemble poetry.' Making allowance for a brief expletive rarely scattered here and there, his poetical language is unadorned, yet rich; select, yet exquisitely plain; condensed, yet homefelt and familiar. He has considered, as he says himself of Parnell, the language of poetry as "the language of life," and conveys the warmest thoughts in the simplest expression.' *Life and Times of Goldsmith*, by JOHN FORSTER.

'The Traveller' was published in 1764, and is interesting as being the first work to which the author attached his name. The poem gives a sketch of the manners and customs of the various countries of Europe, through which the author journeyed on foot, as mentioned in his Life. Goldsmith represents himself as a traveller seated on an Alpine height near a point where Italy, Switzerland and France meet; and thence looking down upon the various lands, he describes their scenery, climate, government, religion and national character, and moralises upon their state and condition. Two great moral lessons stand out in the poem, viz., love of country or patriotism, and the fact that man's happiness does not depend upon country or forms of government, but upon each person's mind or conscience. 'The Traveller,' for which Goldsmith received the sum of only 20 guineas, was highly praised by the critics of the time. Its lively images of varied life, its graceful and simple language, the melody of its verse, and its moral reflections, have made it one of the most popular poems in our language.

*** In the following Notes the term *Old English* is employed in preference to that of *Anglo-Saxon*, because it refers to the language out of which *Modern English* has grown. The term *Anglo-Saxon* is likely to lead young students to imagine that *English* is a different language, which took root in the country to the destruction of *Anglo-Saxon*. This was not the case.

DEDICATION.

TO THE REV. HENRY GOLDSMITH.

Dear Sir,—I am sensible that the friendship between us can acquire no new force from the ceremonies of a dedication; and perhaps it demands an excuse thus to prefix your name to my attempts, which you decline giving with your own. But, as a part of this poem was formerly written to you from Switzerland, the whole can now, with propriety, be only inscribed to you. It will also throw a light upon many parts of it, when the reader understands, that it is addressed to a man who, despising fame and fortune, has retired early to happiness and obscurity, with an income of forty pounds a year.

I now perceive, my dear brother, the wisdom of your humble choice. You have entered upon a sacred office, where the harvest is great, and the labourers are but few; while you have left the field of ambition, where the labourers are many, and the harvest not worth carrying away. But of all kinds of ambition—what from the refinement of the times, from different systems of criticism, and from the divisions of party—that which pursues poetical fame is the wildest. Poetry makes a principal amusement among unpolished nations; but, in a country verging to the extremes of refinement, painting and music come in for a share. As these offer the feeble mind a less laborious entertainment; they at first rival poetry, and at length supplant her; they engross all that favour once shown to her, and though but younger sisters, seize upon the elder's birthright.

Yet, however this art may be neglected by the powerful, it

is still in greater danger from the mistaken efforts of the learned to improve it. What criticisms have we not heard of late in favour of blank verse, and Pindaric odes, choruses, anapaests and iambics, alliterative care and happy negligence! Every absurdity has now a champion to defend it; and as he is generally much in the wrong, so he has always much to say, for error is ever talkative.

But there is an enemy to this art still more dangerous,—I mean party. Party entirely distorts the judgment, and destroys the taste. When the mind is once affected with this disease, it can only find pleasure in what contributes to increase the distemper. Like the tiger, that seldom desists from pursuing man after having once preyed upon human flesh, the reader, who has once gratified his appetite with calumny, makes ever after the most agreeable feast upon murdered reputation. Such readers generally admire some half-witted thing, who wants to be thought a bold man, having lost the character of a wise one. Him they dignify with the name of poet: his tawdry lampoons are called satires; his turbulence is said to be force, and his frenzy fire.[1]

What reception a poem may find, which has neither abuse, party, nor blank verse to support it, I cannot tell, nor am I solicitous to know. My aims are right. Without espousing the cause of any party, I have attempted to moderate the rage of all. I have endeavoured to show, that there may be equal happiness in States that are differently governed from our own; that every State has a particular principle of happiness, and that this principle in each may be carried to a mischievous excess. There are few can judge better than yourself how far these positions are illustrated in this poem.

I am, dear Sir,

Your most affectionate Brother,

OLIVER GOLDSMITH.

[1] Probably in allusion to the poet Churchill, who died 1764.

OLIVER GOLDSMITH.

THE TRAVELLER.

REMOTE, unfriended, melancholy, slow,
Or by the lazy Scheld, or wandering Po;

1 **Remote**, at a distance from home, here used of a person, but commonly of places.

'To men *remote* from power.'—'The Traveller' (437.)

Unfriended, friendless. Friend, now used solely as a noun, was formerly also used as a verb, for which we now employ *befriend*.

'So Fortune *friends* the bold.'
Spenser, 'Faerie Queen.'

'If ever fortune *friend* us with a barque,
Largely supply us with all provision.'
Beaumont and Fletcher, 'Sea Voyage.'

Melancholy, gloomy, dejected (from two Greek words, μέλας, χολή, meaning *black bile*), formerly denoted a kind of moody madness, due to an excess of this fluid mingling with the blood. It was also

Or onward, where the rude Carinthian boor
Against the houseless stranger shuts the door ;
Or where Campania's plain forsaken lies,
A weary waste expanding to the skies ;

used to denote madness in general, and this is its signification in Burton's 'Anatomy of Melancholy.'

'Some *melancholy* men have believed that elephants and birds and other creatures have a language whereby they discourse with one another.'

Reynolds, 'Passions and Faculties of the Soul.'

Slow, referring to the slowness characteristic of a melancholy person (See note A at the end). All the adjs. in this line must be taken with the pronoun **I** in line 7. The order is : 'Where'er I roam,—remote, unfriended, melancholy, slow,– *whether* by the lazy Scheld *or* by the wandering Po.'

2 **Or . . . or.** These words have here the signification of *whether . . . or.* Sometimes in poetry they have also the force of *either . . . or.* But these uses should not be imitated in prose.

'For thy vast bounties are so numberless,
That them *or* to conceal *or* else to tell
Is equally impossible.' Cowley.

Scheld, a river which rises in the north of France and flows through Belgium into the North Sea. Its course is slow, and hence it is termed *lazy.* **Wandering Po.** The Po is a river in the north of Italy, flowing into the Gulf of Venice. Its course being very winding, the poet calls it *wandering.*

3 **Rude,** rough, uncivil, brutal. **Carinthia** is a province of Austria adjoining Italy. **boor.** (Dutch *boer*) means literally merely a cultivator of the soil, a peasant ; then, from the character he is supposed generally to possess, it comes to mean anyone who is rude and unmannerly. The meanings of *knave* a servant, *varlet* a knight's follower, *pagan* a villager, and other words have degenerated in the same way.

4 **Shuts the door.** The poet was thus treated on his visit to Carinthia in 1755.

5 **Campania,** the 'Campagna' of Rome, a dreary plain in the neighbourhood of that city, about sixty miles long and forty

Where'er I roam, whatever realms to see,
My heart untravelled fondly turns to thee;
Still to my brother turns, with ceaseless pain,
And drags at each remove a lengthening chain.

Eternal blessings crown my earliest friend,
And round his dwelling guardian saints attend!

wide. It abounds with swamps, which produce a pestilential *malaria*. The inhabitants of this tract of country suffer much, and have all the appearance of persons afflicted with dropsy, jaundice, and ague. Its population is therefore comparatively small, and it is usually avoided by tourists, especially at certain seasons of the year. Hence the poet calls it *forsaken*.

6 **Expanding to the skies,** i.e. so extensive as to be bounded only by the horizon.

7 **Heart untravelled,** left at home, not travelling with its owner. A metaphorical expression. (See line 10.)

8 **Fondly,** affectionately. Fond formerly meant foolish, silly. 'A *fond* thing, vainly invented.'—*Articles of the Church of England, No. xxii.*
Bishop Barrow in one of his sermons describes a profane swearer as a *fondling*. So Shakespeare—

> 'And for his dreams, I wonder he is so *fond*,
> To trust the mockery of unquiet slumbers.'
>
> Richard III. iii. 2.

to thee, referring to his brother Henry, to whom the author dedicated the poem. Cf. 'Citizen of the World,' Let. iii.

9 **Still,** always, continually. This word denotes a continuance of any state or condition, whether of rest or motion.

10 **A lengthening chain.** A metaphorical allusion to the fact that the longer a chain is, the heavier it is. The farther he went from his brother, the heavier his heart became.

11 **Crown.** This is the optative use of the verb, expressing a wish, 'May eternal blessings crown.'

12 **Guardian saints,** i.e. guardian angels. **attend,** be on the watch to avert danger. Optative (11).

Blest be that spot, where cheerful guests retire
To pause from toil and trim their evening fire!
Blest that abode, where want and pain repair,
And every stranger finds a ready chair!
Blest be those feasts with simple plenty crowned,
Where all the ruddy family around

13 **Blest.** The past tense and the past participle of the verb *to bless* are usually written *blessed*, especially in prose. *Blest*, however, a contraction of *blessed*, is common enough in poetry. Cf. 'Blessed are the merciful,' Matt. v. 7.

> '*Blest* is the man who ne'er consents
> By ill advice to walk.'
>
> Psalm 1, 'Metrical Version.'

15 **Where** is here put for *whither*, the proper word to denote motion to a place. *Where* strictly expresses rest in a place. **want and pain**, abstract for concrete, i.e. for poor and suffering persons. **repair**, go to, resort to: a different word entirely from *repair*, to mend, which comes through the French from the Lat. *reparare*, to prepare again. The former word comes through the French from a non-classical Lat. word *repatriare*, to return to one's country.

16 **A ready chair,** i.e. he was always welcome.

17 **Simple plenty,** plenty of food of a plain and *simple*, not luxurious, kind. *Simple* is connected with the Lat. *simplex*, and means literally once folded; from *sim = semel*, once, and *plico, -atum*, to fold.

18 **Ruddy**, approaching to redness, pale red, rosy.

Rud is an O.E. word meaning redness, a blush.

> 'Fast, with a redd *rudd*,
> To her chamber can shee flee.'
>
> Boy and Mantle, 'Percy's Reliques.'

Hence, *ruddle*, red earth, red ochre; *Rut*land, so named from the redness of the soil; and *ruddock*, little red one, which was a common name with the older poets for the Redbreast.

Laugh at the jests or pranks that never fail,
Or sigh with pity at some mournful tale;
Or press the bashful stranger to his food,
And learn the luxury of doing good!

But me, not destined such delights to share,
My prime of life in wandering spent and care,
Impelled with steps unceasing to pursue
Some fleeting good, that mocks me with the view,

Prank, a ludicrous trick, a mischievous act. This word was once employed in the sense of ostentatious display:—hence our word *prance*, to which it is allied. Cf.

> 'Some *prancke* their ruffles.'
> Spenser, 'Faerie Queen,' i. iv, 14.

> 'That ever I this dismal day did see!
> Full far was I from thinking such a *pranke*.'
> Ibid., v. 1, 15.

Where the word means a mischievous and cruel act, as the context shows.

19 **Jest,** originally, exploit, deed, from Lat. *gero, gestum*, to do, carry on, wage (war). Hence anything interesting or amusing.

22 **The luxury of doing good.** Cf.

> 'The quality of Mercy is not strain'd.
> It blesseth him that gives and him that takes.'
> Shakespeare, 'Merchant of Venice.'

23 **Me,** objective after leads; line 29.

24 **Prime,** from the Latin *primus*, first, means the first part, the beginning, and hence, the best part, the spring of life, height of health, strength, or beauty. *prim*rose, lit. the first rose. *prim*er, lit. a first book. **and care,** i.e. and in care. The order is: 'My prime of life being spent in wandering and in care.'

26 **Fleeting,** passing swiftly away.

Mocks me with the view. The poet probably had in his

That, like the circle bounding earth and skies,
Allures from far, yet, as I follow, flies:
My fortune leads to traverse realms alone,
And find no spot of all the world my own.

E'en now, where Alpine solitudes ascend,
I sit me down a pensive hour to spend;

mind the phenomenon of the Mirage. The realisation of an anticipated pleasure is often disappointing. Cf.

> 'Hope springs eternal in the human breast,
> Man never *is*, but always *to be*, blest.'
>
> Pope, 'Essay on Man,' i. 95.

26 **Good.** This word, really, an adj., often becomes a noun, as is shown by its taking the plural form, *goods*, although with a slightly different meaning. This change is called 'conversion.' Compare *black, blacks; ill, ills; sweet, sweets; bitter, bitters.* Other adjectives, although frequently used without nouns, as *poor, bad, blind, deaf, dumb, wicked, idle*, &c., are not converted into nouns, as is shown by their not taking the plural form.

27 **The circle**, the horizon, which, in consequence of the earth's shape, bounds the view on all sides and is never the nearer, however we may apparently go towards it.

29 **Leads**, i.e. leads **me** (23). **alone**, qualifies **me**.

31 **E'en.** The young reader must observe that in such abbreviated words as e'en, e'er, ne'er, sha'n't, can't, &c., the apostrophe must always be placed where the letter or letters are left out. The contraction of a word by taking out one or more letters from the middle of it is called *Syncope* (Greek, a cutting short), and it is then said to be *syncopated*. *Elision* is a word of Latin origin, meaning the cutting a syllable off, or out from, a word.

31 **Alpine solitudes**, among the Alps in Switzerland, or any similarly lofty mountains.

> 'Palmy shades and aromatick woods,
> That grace the plains, invest the peopled hills,
> And up the more than *Alpine* mountains wave.'
>
> Thomson, 'Summer.'

And, placed on high above the storm's career,
Look downward where a hundred realms appear :
Lakes, forests, cities, plains extending wide,
The pomp of kings, the shepherd's humbler pride.

'Some vague emotion of delight
In gazing up an *Alpine* height,
Some yearning toward the lamps of night.'
Tennyson, 'The Two Voices.'

32 **Sit me**, an example of the Old English way of adding the personal pronoun after many verbs both neuter and active. Cf. the forms, 'I will *lay me* down,' Ps. iv 8. 'I *hie me* home.'

'My will is even this,
That presently you *hie you* home to bed.'
Shakespeare, 'Two Gentlemen of Verona,' iv. 2.

These may be called reflected personal pronouns.

33 **Above the storm's career**. It is often calm in the upper regions of the air when it is tempestuous in the lower; and in mountainous countries, travellers on the hills frequently see the storms raging in the valleys below them while the sky is serene above.

'As some tall cliff that lifts its awful form,
Swells from the vale, *and midway leaves the storm*,
Though round its breast the rolling clouds are spread,
Eternal sunshine settles on its head.'
Goldsmith, 'Deserted Village,' 189.

'Though *far below* the forkèd lightnings play,
And *at his feet* the thunder dies away.'
Rogers, 'Pleasures of Memory.'

Career, lit. a road for a car (Lat. *carrus*), from French *carrière*.

'They had run themselves too far out of breath, to go back again the same *career*.' Sir Philip Sidney.

34 **Hundred**, used indefinitely for a large number.

36 **The pomp of kings**, &c., i.e. the view takes in kings' palaces as well as shepherds' cottages. *Pomp* (Gr. πομπή, Lat. pompa; from Gr. πέμπω, to send), meant originally an escort, and thence, a grand procession, display of grandeur.

When thus creation's charms around combine,
Amidst the store should thankless pride repine?
Say, should the philosophic mind disdain
That good which makes each humbler bosom vain?
Let school-taught pride dissemble all it can,
These little things are great to little man;
And wiser he whose sympathetic mind
Exults in all the good of all mankind.
Ye glittering towns with wealth and splendour crowned;
Ye fields where summer spreads profusion round;
Ye lakes whose vessels catch the busy gale;
Ye bending swains that dress the flowery vale;
For me your tributary stores combine,
Creation's heir, the world, the world is mine!

37 **Creation.** This word is not here used in its *abstract* sense, the work of creating, but in its *concrete* sense, that which has been created, i.e. the Universe.

38 **Store,** abundance, Old Fr. *estoire.* Lat. *instauro,* to renew.

39 **Philosophic,** reasoning, enquiring into cause and effect. **disdain,** despise the humbler pleasures of others.

40 **That good** (26).

41 **School-taught,** i.e. taught in the schools of philosophy. All philosophers of the Middle Ages were called 'Schoolmen.' **Dissemble,** to pretend that that which really is, is not. Lat. *dissimulo,* to disguise or conceal.

43 **Sympathetic,** having a kindly feeling with and for others. Sympathy is derived from the Greek, and = Lat. *compassion.* **Wiser,** i.e. than philosophers.

47 **Lakes,** Geneva, Lucerne, Zurich, Constance, &c., in the neighbourhood of the Alps. **busy,** occupied in filling the sails of the ships.

48 **Bending swains,** labourers at work in the fields. **dress** (Fr. *dresser,* from Lat. *dirigo,* to make straight), to prepare land for crops. 'And the Lord God took the man, and put him into the garden of Eden to *dress* it and to keep it.' Gen. ii. 15.

> 'Well must the ground be digg'd and better *dress'd,*
> New soil to make and meliorate the rest.' Dryden.

As some lone miser, visiting his store,
Bends at his treasure, counts, recounts it o'er;
Hoards after hoards his rising raptures fill,
Yet still he sighs, for hoards are wanting still:
Thus to my breast alternate passions rise,
Pleased with each good that Heaven to man supplies;

50 **Heir**, in apposition to **me** (49).
Cowper, in 'The Task, Winter Morning,' says:—

> 'He looks abroad into the varied field
> Of Nature; and though poor, perhaps, compared
> With those whose mansions glitter in his sight,
> Calls the delightful scenery *all his own*.'

Cf. also 1 Cor. iii. 22.

51 **Miser** is from the Lat. adj. *miser*, wretched, denoting the character and disposition of the man who hoards up, instead of making a good use of, his wealth. The words *miser*, *misery*, and *miserable* have reversed their uses. *Miser* formerly meant simply a wretched person, but now a covetous one; *misery* meant covetousness, now it means wretchedness; *miserable* meant covetous, but now, wretched.

> 'Vouchsafe to stay your steed for humble *miser's* sake.'
> Spenser, 'Faerie Queen,' ii. 1, 8.

'Perseus returned again to his old humour, which was born and bred with him, and that was avarice and *misery*.'
North's 'Plutarch's Lives.

'The liberal-hearted man is, by the opinion of the prodigal, *miserable*; and by the judgment of the *miserable*, lavish.'
Hooker, 'Ecclesiastical Polity,' v. 5.

52 **Recounts**, literally, counts again.

53 **His rising raptures fill**, i.e. give him the greater pleasure, the more hoards he sees.

54 **Wanting**. This is the active participle used in a passive sense for 'being wanted,' a common usage due to the absence of a true present participle passive in English. Cf. 'The house is *building*.' 'The book is *printing*.' 'The goods are *selling*,' &c.

55 **Alternate**, changing, varying, first one and then another. **passions**. Passion (Lat. *patior*, *passus*, to suffer) is properly any

Yet oft a sigh prevails, and sorrows fall,
To see the hoard of human bliss so small;
And oft I wish, amidst the scene, to find
Some spot to real happiness consigned,
Where my worn soul, each wandering hope at rest,
May gather bliss, to see my fellows blest.

But, where to find that happiest spot below,
Who can direct, when all pretend to know?
The shuddering tenant of the frigid zone
Boldly proclaims that happiest spot his own;
Extols the treasures of his stormy seas,
And his long nights of revelry and ease;

effect produced upon the mind by external agency, and which the mind therefore *suffers*. Then it comes to mean any violent commotion of the mind, such as love, anger, zeal, suffering, &c.

57 **Prevails,** gets the mastery. **sorrows fall,** i.e. upon the heart.

60 **Consigned,** given up to.

61 **Each wandering hope at rest,** i.e. being at rest. The construction of *hope* here is called the nominative absolute, since there is no verb to which it is subject. In all absolute constructions in English, one of the words is either a substantive or a pronoun, the other a participle.

62 **To see,** i.e. *from*, or *by* seeing. **blest** (13).

63 **To find,** inf. after *direct* (64).

64 **Direct.** Supply *me*.

65 **Tenant,** inhabitant. **frigid zone.** There are two frigid zones, the North, bounded by the Arctic Circle, 23° 28′ S. of the North Pole; and the South bounded by the Antarctic Circle, 23° 28′ N. of the South Pole. The North frigid zone is here alluded to; the South having never been explored to any great extent. But the latter is believed to be uninhabited, as it is much colder than the former, and no traces of vegetation have ever been found there. *Frigid zone* in the text, however, is used generally, for the coldest portion of the earth.

66 **That happiest spot,** i.e. that his own country is the best in the world.

The naked negro, panting at the line,
Boasts of his golden sands and palmy wine,
Basks in the glare, or stems the tepid wave,
And thanks his gods for all the good they gave.

Such is the patriot's boast, where'er we roam,
His first, best country, ever is at home.

67 **Treasures,** Whales, seals, walruses, &c.

68 **Long nights** In winter the sun's rays do not fall within the frigid zone; but in summer, the sun is always above the horizon, consequently, in those portions of the earth, summer is one long day and winter one long night. In the most northern parts of Europe, the sun does not rise above the horizon between November 20 and January 10

69 **Panting** breathing rapidly on account of the heat. **line,** the Equator, or Equinoctial Line, so called because places on it have equal nights, and consequently equal days, throughout the year. It is the hottest part of the earth's surface, since there the sun is always immediately overhead at midday.

70 **Golden sands** Gold was formerly an important article of export from the central African coast. The coin called a *guinea* was so named because first made of gold brought from the coast of Guinea. **Palmy wine** Wine obtained from the fruit or the sap of a palm tree. There are about 600 different species of palms. Most of the African varieties yield excellent wine, especially the Palmyra and the cocoa-nut palms.

71 **Stems the tepid wave** Tepid means lukewarm, warm in a small degree. The negroes and the inhabitants of the various islands in the Pacific learn the art of swimming in infancy. **glare,** hot, bright light of the sun. The word is connected with the English *clear* and Lat. *clarus.*

72 **Gave,** have given.

74 **His first, best country,** i.e. in his opinion. Longfellow's Poem, 'The happiest land,' enters into this subject. Cf.—

'Breathes there the man with soul so dead
Who never to himself hath said,
This is my own, my native land!'
Scott, 'Lay of the Last Minstrel.'

And yet, perhaps, if countries we compare,
And estimate the blessings which they share,
Though patriots flatter, still shall wisdom find
An equal portion dealt to all mankind ;
As different good, by art or nature given,
To different nations makes their blessings even.

Nature, a mother kind alike to all,
Still grants her bliss at labour's earnest call ;
With food as well the peasant is supplied
On Idra's cliffs as Arno's shelvy side ;

78 **An equal portion**, i.e. of blessings (75).

79 **As**, since, because. **good** (26). **by art or nature,** i.e. *whether* by art *or* by nature (2)

80 **Makes their blessings even**. The possession of one blessing compensates for the want of another.

82 **Still** 9). **at labour's earnest call** Though Nature produces many blessings spontaneously, yet it is only by earnest labour, i.e. cultivation of the land, working mines, &c., that she bestows her richest and most abundant blessings upon men.

83 **As well**. The order is : 'The peasant is as well supplied with food on Idra's cliffs as on Arno's shelvy side.' Not 'on Idra's cliffs *as well as* on Arno's shelvy side.' **peasant**, a countryman, rustic. French *paysan*, from *pays*, the country, Lat. *pagus*, whence *pagan*, a villager.

84 **Idra** (properly Idria), a town in Carniola, a district of Illyria (Austria), is situated in a hollow hemmed in by wooded mountains, and is celebrated for its quicksilver mines. Hydra is a rocky island of Greece, east of the Morea. **Arno**, a river of Tuscany in Italy. **Shelvy**, shallow, rocky, full of banks or shelves The word is sometimes written *shelfy*.

> 'Glides by the sirens' cliffs, a *shelfy* coast
> Long infamous for ships and sailors lost,
> And white with bones.'
>
> Dryden, 'Trans. of Æneid, v. 1125.

It appears to mean *rocky* in the following passage :--

'The tillable fields are in some places so tough that the plough will

And though the rocky-crested summits frown,
These rocks, by custom, turn to beds of down.
From art more various are the blessings sent,—
Wealth, commerce, honour, liberty, content.
Yet these each other's power so strong contest,
That either seems destructive of the rest.

scarcely cut them: and in some so *shelfy* that the corn hath much ado to fasten its root.'—Carew, 'Survey of Cornwall.'

85 **Frown,** Cf.

> 'The castled crag of Drachenfels
> *Frowns* o'er the wide and winding Rhine.'
> Byron, 'Childe Harold,' iii.

86 **Turn to beds of down,** i.e. the inhabitants of these regions are so accustomed to sleeping on the hard rocks, that they rest as comfortably there as others do on beds of down. We must make allowance for some poetical exaggeration here. **down,** fine soft feathers.'

87 The order is: 'The blessings sent from art are more various.' Blessings, i.e. comforts produced by artificial, not natural, means are alluded to.

88 **Wealth, commerce,** &c. These words are all in apposition to *blessings* in the line above. **content,** contentment. Cf.

> Nought's had, all's spent,
> Where our desire is got without *content*.'
> Shakespeare, 'Macbeth,' iii. 2.

89 **Strong,** adj. for adv. strongly (261). **contest,** commonly a neuter verb, is here used in an active sense, meaning to dispute, controvert, call in question; as in the following passage:—

''Tis evident, upon what account none have presumed to *contest* the proposition of these ancient pieces.'—Dryden, 'Trans. of Dufresnoy's Art of Painting.' As a neuter verb, it is usually followed by *with*—

'The difficulty of an argument adds to the pleasure of *contesting with it*, when there are hopes of victory.'—Bishop Burnet.

90 **Either,** properly one of two, but here, any one of them which may be taken. **destructive of the rest.** The poet means that wealth is destructive of content in often producing

Where wealth and freedom reign, contentment fails,
And honour sinks where commerce long prevails.
Hence every state, to one loved blessing prone,
Conforms and models life to that alone.
Each to the favourite happiness attends,
And spurns the plan that aims at other ends;
Till carried to excess in each domain,
This favourite good begets peculiar pain.

But let us try these truths with closer eyes,
And trace them through the prospect as it lies.
Here, for a while my proper cares resigned,
Here let me sit in sorrow for mankind,

avarice; that commerce is destructive of honour, because in too many cases those engaged in trade care for nothing so long as they can make money; and so on. His statement, however, must be received with considerable reservation.

91 This and the following line are explanatory of the assertion made in 89 and 90, and are not contained in the earlier editions of the poem.

93 **Hence every state,** &c., i.e. the mercantile state makes everything subservient to commerce, the wealthy state to wealth. **prone,** inclined, literally, bending forwards, Lat. *pronus.*

96 **Spurns,** casts aside, rejects with disdain.

97 **Domain,** usually an estate: here, the country. Fr. *demesne* (pr. demain), Lat. *dominium,* an estate, from *dominus,* a lord or master, and that again from *domus,* a house.

98 **Geo I** (26). **peculiar pain.** Thus excess of wealth produces luxuriousness of living. Excess of commercial enterprise lowers public honour. So liberty is apt to degenerate into license, and contentment to indolent acquiescence in things as they are, however bad they may be.

99 **Try,** &c., examine them more carefully.

100 **Trace,** i.e. let us trace. **as it lies,** i.e. before me (33, 34).

101 **Proper,** own, peculiar to oneself. Fr. *propre,* Lat. *proprius.*

Like yon neglected shrub, at random cast,
That shades the steep, and sighs at every blast.

Far to the right, where Apennine ascends,
Bright as the summer, Italy extends :
Its uplands sloping deck the mountain's side,
Woods over woods in gay theatric pride ;
While oft some temple's mouldering tops between
With venerable grandeur mark the scene.

Could nature's bounty satisfy the breast,
The sons of Italy were surely blest.

103 **Shrub at random cast**, a solitary shrub on the side of the hill, which has been planted there no one knows how.

104 **Sighs at every blast**, lest it should be torn up by the roots : an example of Hyperbole.

105 **Far to the right.** The poet represents himself as sitting on the side of some mountain (32) west of Italy, *facing the east*, in which case, of course, the Apennines, a range of mountains running the whole length of Italy, would be on his right hand.

106 **Italy**, in South of Europe, famous for its blue skies and delightful climate.

107 **Its uplands sloping.** Uplands is here nominative to deck. Sloping is a present participle qualifying uplands, with which 'woods over woods' appears to be in apposition. If the comma were placed (as in some editions) after *sloping* instead of after *side*, 'uplands sloping' would be nominative absolute (61) and 'woods over woods' nominative to deck. The punctuation in the text is that of the ninth and last edition published during the author's lifetime. *Theatric*, as in a theatre, probably refers to the trees 'woods over woods,' like the spectators in a theatre, especially in the old Roman Amphitheatres. The woods which formerly covered the sides of the Apennines have now, for the most part, been cut down.

109 **Between**, i.e. between the woods.

110 **Venerable grandeur.** Numerous ruins of ancient temples are, of course, met with in a classic land like Italy.

111 **Could Nature's bounty**, i.e. if it could.

112 **Were**, subjunctive mood, = would be.

Whatever fruits in different climes are found,
That proudly rise, or humbly court the ground;
Whatever blooms in torrid tracts appear,
Whose bright succession decks the varied year;
Whatever sweets salute the northern sky
With vernal lives, that blossom but to die;
These, here disporting, own the kindred soil,
Nor ask luxuriance from the planter's toil;

113 **Climes**, is here put for countries by Metonymy.

114 **That proudly rise**, that grow on lofty trees. **court the ground**, i.e. trail on it, as the pumpkin, vegetable marrow, &c. Among the fruits of Italy may be mentioned the orange, lemon, olive, carob, pomegranate, date, custard apple, grape, chestnut, mulberry, pistachio, apple, pear, apricot, and jujube. The sugar-cane, maize, and rice are also cultivated, besides wheat and other kinds of corn. Among those which 'humbly court the ground,' may be mentioned the caper, which grows like the bramble, and the flower-buds of which form an important article of export.

115 **Torrid**, very hot. The Torrid Zone (65) extends 23° 28′ on each side of the Equator (66), being bounded on the N. by the Tropic of Cancer, and on the S. by the Tropic of Capricorn, and is commonly known as 'The Tropics.' **tracts**. *tract* is from the Lat. *traho, tractum* (frequentative, *tracto, tractatum*), to draw, and is applied to an account *drawn up* in the form of a little book (called also tractate), as well as to an extent of country, *drawn* or stretched out.

117 **Sweets**, perfumes of flowers: an example of Conversion. Cf. *good* (26). The flowers of temperate climates have usually a sweeter perfume than those of warmer ones.

118 **Vernal**, lasting only during the spring, from the Lat. *ver*, spring. **lives** is here a noun. **but to die**, the flowers of the hawthorn, violet, lilac, rose, lily of the valley, &c., fade very quickly.

119 **Own**, acknowledge, confess, not deny. The sense is, 'These fruits and flowers, by their natural luxuriance, *acknowledge* that the soil is of a kind suited to them.' Cf.

'Others will *own* their weakness of understanding.'—Locke.

While sea-born gales their gelid wings expand
To winnow fragrance round the smiling land.

But small the bliss that sense alone bestows,
And sensual bliss is all this nation knows.
In florid beauty groves and fields appear,
Man seems the only growth that dwindles here.

The word *own*, to possess, is an entirely different word, being derived from the O.E. *agan*, to possess, whilst the former is from *unnan*, to give, bestow, grant. **kindred.** This is the *predicative* use of the adjective. Its position before the noun is very unusual, and is only justified by the exigence of the verse. *Kindred*, is derived from the O.E., *kin*, relationship, and in this sense, the word *kindred*, as a noun, is now generally used. Cf. 238.

120 **Nor ask luxuriance,** &c., i.e. do not require to be cultivated. They grow *wild* in great luxuriance and perfection.

121 **Sea-born gales,** breezes from the sea. **gelid.** generally means cold, frosty, but here merely cool and refreshing. **wings,** the poet seems to speak of the sea-breezes as angels rising from the sea and flying over the land. It is a happy and beautiful idea, since sea-breezes are as a rule refreshing and healthful, especially in warm climates, whilst land-breezes are generally the reverse.

122 **Winnow.** to separate by means of the wind, especially chaff from grain. It appears to be here used simply in the sense of to waft. **fragrance,** the perfumes of flowers and trees.

123 **Sense,** the senses generally. Sensation, perception by any one of the senses.

124 **Sensual bliss,** i.e., the happiness conferred through the medium of the senses, hearing, feeling, smelling, tasting, and seeing. The poet says, they confer only a *small amount* of bliss. He is wrong here. The *quantity* of this kind of bliss is great, for it is common to all animals, but it is the lowest *kind* of bliss.

125 **Florid,** gay with flowers, bright in colour, embellished. The word, is now commonly used to denote excess of colour or ornament. **grove.** O.E. *graef*, from *grafan*, to dig, because it was hollowed out of a thicket of trees, and did not apply to the thicket itself. In modern English it applies to both. Grave (a dug-out place) graving, engrave, are all derived from the same root.

Contrasted faults through all his manners reign :
Though poor, luxurious ; though submissive, vain ;
Though grave, yet trifling ; zealous, yet untrue ;
And e'en in penance planning sins anew.
All evils here contaminate the mind,
That opulence departed leaves behind ;
For wealth was theirs, not far removed the date,
When commerce proudly flourished through the state ;

126 **The only growth.** The poet means that whilst vegetation in Italy flourishes, the inhabitants degenerate. This is true, for they are in character and wealth very inferior to what they formerly were (133–138).

127 **Contrasted faults.** This expression is explained in the following lines, where poverty is contrasted with luxury ; submission with vanity ; gravity with pettiness ; zeal with deceit. **manners,** the actions resulting from his moral character, something more than mere *manners*, as the term is now used.

129 **Zealous**, full of zeal for religion. 'The Spectator' says a zealous man will often find that what he calls a Zeal for his Religion is either Pride, Interest, or Ill-nature. No. 185, an Essay well worth reading.

130 **Penance**, a punishment undergone as an expression of sorrow for sin, and properly therefore, voluntary. Formerly, however, it meant *repentance* as well.

'Seeking to bring forth worthy fruits of *penance*.'—Book of Common Prayer, 'The Commination.'

The poet means that whilst the Italians voluntarily undergo penance for past sins, they are so insincere that they at the same time plan the commission of fresh ones.

131 **All evils here.** &c. The order is : 'All evils here, that departed opulence leaves behind, contaminate the mind.' Thus they learnt habits of luxury in their opulence which they continue to indulge in their poverty (128). Though their poverty now compels them to be submissive, they are as vain as when they were rich.

133 **For wealth was theirs.** *Was* is here emphatic. **not far removed the date,** i.e. in comparatively recent times *Date* is from the Lat. *do, datum*, to give, and means the

At her command the palace learned to rise,
Again the long-fall'n column sought the skies,
The canvas glowed, beyond e'en nature warm,
The pregnant quarry teemed with human form ;
Till, more unsteady than the southern gale,
Commerce on other shores displayed her sail ;

time when any law or other writing was *datum*, given. Cf. the form now used in official documents : '*Given* under our hand and seal this (21st) day of, &c. &c.'

134 **Commerce proudly flourished.** Towards the close of the 15th century, Italy was at its highest point of prosperity Venice was the most important commercial state of Italy for many centuries. Florence, Genoa, and Pisa were also celebrated for their commercial prosperity and refinement.

135. **At her command**, i.e. at the command of Commerce. The merchants of Italy, and especially of Venice, built magnificent palaces.

136 **The long fall'n column sought the skies.** This may be taken almost literally. The marble columns of ancient Rome and other Italian cities, which had been thrown down or had fallen from neglect, were re-erected.

137 **The canvas glowed.** Painting flourished. The Italians have long been famous as painters and sculptors. *Canvas* is derived from the Lat. *cannabis*, hemp, through the French *canevas*. The cloth made from hemp was, and is, much used for painting on with oil colours. **beyond e'en nature warm.** The colours on the canvas were warmer and more brilliant even than the natural ones, which were more than imitated. *Titian*, an Italian painter, who lived in the end of the 15th and beginning of the 16th century, was noted for warmth of colouring.

138 **Pregnant quarry.** The finest marble for sculpture is found in Italy. **teem'd with human form.** *To teem* is to be filled with a thing. The poet alludes to the idea that in the unhewn block of marble the figure to be carved out of it lies, and that it becomes visible when the superfluous stone is removed.

139 **Southern gale.** This wind, called the Sirocco, comes across the deserts of Africa, and is the most changeable of all the winds which blow in Italy.

While nought remained of all that riches gave,
But towns unmanned and lords without a slave:
And late the nation found with fruitless skill
Its former strength was but plethoric ill.

Yet still the loss of wealth is here supplied
By arts, the splendid wrecks of former pride;
From these the feeble heart and long-fallen mind
An easy compensation seem to find.
Here may be seen, in bloodless pomp arrayed,
The pasteboard triumph and the cavalcade;

140 **Other shores**, owing partly to the discovery of new countries. America was discovered in 1492. **displayed her sail.** This is a strictly poetical expression, for, 'Commercial enterprise forsook Italy and went to other lands.'

142 **Towns unmanned**, i.e. depopulated, deprived of inhabitants.

143 **Skill**, knowledge. **Fruitless**, because it came too late to be of use.

144 **Plethoric**, having a full habit. The allusion is to a man who is diseased from a superabundance of blood in his veins. From the Greek πλήθω (plēthō) I am full, πληθώρη (plēthōrē) fulness.

146 **Splendid wrecks.** Painting and sculpture. The latter was practised with great success by the ancient Romans, and the former by the Romans, Venetians, and others of the Middle Ages. The poet considers the present condition of Art in Italy a mere *wreck* of what it once was. **Fallen mind**, depraved, debased.

148 **Easy compensation.** Their minds and tastes being debased, they are satisfied with inferior works of art.

150 **Pasteboard triumph.** In old Roman times, grand processions or 'triumphs' were decreed to victorious generals as a mark of honour. The poet speaks of *bloodless pomp* because no blood has been shed, and no wounded prisoners are seen in the processions now. The *pasteboard triumph* refers to the decorations, and pasteboard imitations of trophies, used in the processions of the Carnival season at Rome. Pasteboard was originally made by

5 Give in your own language the substance of [illegible]. Narrating [illegible] the [illegible] of [illegible] lates and [illegible] the [illegible]

[illegible]

Why has the poet [illegible] the [illegible] [illegible] [illegible] [illegible] [illegible] [illegible] [illegible] from [illegible] [illegible] scenery

Point out the [illegible] [illegible] [illegible]

Processions formed for piety and love,
A mistress or a saint in every grove.
By sports like these are all their cares beguiled;
The sports of children satisfy the child;
Each nobler aim, represt by long control,
Now sinks at last, or feebly mans the soul;
While low delights, succeeding fast behind,
In happier meanness occupy the mind:
As in those domes, where Cæsars once bore sway,
Defaced by time and tottering in decay,

pasting various thicknesses of paper together. The Carnival (Lat. *caro, carnis,* flesh: *vale,* farewell) is held just before Lent, during which season flesh is not eaten by devout Roman Catholics. *Pasteboard triumph,* however, may mean merely a *sham* one. **cavalcade,** a procession on horseback, perhaps referring to the races of horses without riders held in the Corso at Rome during the Carnival.

151 **Processions**. These words, *triumph, cavalcade, processions, mistress, saint,* are all nominatives to *may be seen.*

154 **The sports of children**. Sir Joshua Reynolds, visiting Goldsmith one day, found the poet teaching his dog to beg. On the table lay the unfinished manuscript of 'The Traveller,' with the ink of this line still wet. **beguiled,** deceived in a pleasing manner, driven away with amusement.

155 **Represt by long control.** The allusion is to that of a man of noble and ambitious spirit being kept in subjection until that spirit is broken, or, at least, deprived of its elasticity and energy.

156 **Mans the soul**. The allusion is to a garrison *manned* with troops, or a ship *manned* with sailors. As these have no strength, when *unmanned,* to resist the foe, or to attack him, so the soul when *unmanned,* or feebly *manned,* is the more open to temptation and the less able to resist it.

157 **Fast,** an adv. = rapidly.

159 **Domes**. A *dome* is properly any house, from the Lat. *domus,* a house, but is here applied to palaces. How it came to be applied to a *cupola,* the sense in which it is now commonly used, is uncertain. **Caesars**. The Roman Emperors who adopted the

There in the ruin, heedless of the dead,
The shelter-seeking peasant builds his shed;
And, wondering man could want the larger pile,
Exults, and owns his cottage with a smile.

My soul, turn from them, turn we to survey
Where rougher climes a nobler race display,
Where the bleak Swiss their stormy mansion tread,
And force a churlish soil for scanty bread,

title from Julius Cæsar. The German *Kaiser* and the Russian *Czar* are different forms of the same word.

161 **Heedless of the dead.** Not regarding them, not thinking of them.

162 **Builds his shed.** The peasants of Italy frequently build their huts among the ruins of palaces.

163 **Wondering man,** i.e. wondering *that* man could want, &c.

164 **With a smile,** at the thought that anyone should have built so large a palace, whilst so small a hut satisfies him.

166 **Rougher climes.** Climates less soft and luxurious than that of Italy.

167 **Bleak Swiss.** The adjective *bleak* is here transferred from the country to its inhabitants. *Bleak* now means cold, chill, cheerless; but formerly it meant *pale.*

'You look ill, methinks, have you been sick of late?
Troth, very *bleak*; doth she not?'
Middleton, 'Witch,' iii. 2.

'When she came out, she looked as pale and as *bleak* as one th[illegible] were laid out dead.'

Foxe, 'Book of Martyrs; The Escape of Agnes Wardall.'

This word is the same as the O. E. *blæc*, black. *Bleak, black,* and *bleach* are all connected, being derived from a root which signified loss of natural colour. If Goldsmith intended the adj. *bleak* to be applied to the people, he used it in its obsolete sense of *pale* as compared with the somewhat darker complexioned Italians.

[illegible]

[illegible]

25. [illegible] Smith says the [illegible]
states are [illegible] contend[illegible]
freedom [illegible]
he says [illegible] their pleasures [illegible]
because their wants are [illegible]
That science flies from them
and when [illegible] other [illegible]
[illegible] they have [illegible]
to delight them.
The powers that [illegible]
unknown [illegible] them or if they [illegible]
[illegible] some high [illegible]
[illegible] and punish [illegible]

too early bound

not engaged … things

D'Alembert

303 to 310

No product here the barren hills afford
But man and steel, the soldier and his sword;
No vernal blooms their torpid rocks array,
But winter lingering chills the lap of May;

No zephyr fondly sues the mountain's breast,
But meteors glare, and stormy glooms invest.

mansion from the Lat. *maneo, mansum,* to stay, now used only of a large house, was formerly applied to any.

> 'There, where a few torn shrubs the place disclose,
> The village preacher's modest *mansion* rose.'
> Goldsmith, 'Deserted Village.'

In the text it is used for country.

168 **Force a churlish soil.** The soil of Switzerland is naturally very barren compared with that of Italy, and, therefore, requires much labour to be expended upon it. **churlish** is from an O.E. word *ceorl*, a rustic, a countryman, a labourer; and hence means uncultivated, rude, rough, uncivil; and as applied to things, unmanageable, vexatious.

> 'In the hundreds of Essex they have a very *churlish* blue clay.'
> Mortimer, 'Husbandry.'

170 **But man and steel.** The Swiss have for centuries enlisted in large numbers in the military service of foreign Powers.

171 **Vernal blooms**, spring flowers. **torpid**, sleepy, lifeless; as incapable of maintaining even vegetable life. **array**, deck, dress, clothe. Goldsmith forgot the Alpine roses and the gentians, the abundance and beauty of which, on the Alps, never fail to arrest the attention and admiration of the traveller.

172 **Winter lingering chills**, &c. These lines are highly poetical and beautiful. The winter lasts longer among the mountains of Switzerland than in Italy, because of their greater elevation and higher latitude.

173 **Zephyr**, the name given by the Ancient Greeks to any westerly wind, and often spoken of as a god. In Europe, west winds are warmer than either the north or east, because they blow

Yet still, even here, content can spread a charm,
Redress the clime, and all its rage disarm.
Though poor the peasant's hut, his feast though small,
He sees his little lot the lot of all;
Sees no contiguous palace rear its head
To shame the meanness of his humble shed;
No costly lord the sumptuous banquet deal,
To make him loathe his vegetable meal;
But calm, and bred in ignorance and toil,
Each wish contracting, fits him to the soil.

from the sea, which, in winter, has a higher temperature than the land.

174 **Meteors,** falling or shooting stars, as they are generally called. The name meteor, however, which is derived from a Greek word meaning aloft, is applied also to lightning, the Aurora Borealis, mock suns, clouds, waterspouts, hurricanes, and other phenomena of the upper regions. **stormy glooms,** owing to the sun being obscured by clouds. **invest,** lit. to cover up with a robe, Lat. *in*, in, and *vestis*, a garment.

176 **Redress the clime,** make up for the unfavourable character of the climate.

179 **Contiguous,** close by, almost touching. **palace,** Fr. *palais*, Lat. *palatium*, from the name of one of the Seven hills of Rome, generally called the Palatine Hill, on which the residence of the Emperor Augustus was built.

181 **Costly lord.** *Costly* here may mean merely sumptuous, splendid, grand; or that the lord is *costly* to the peasant who has to pay rent or taxes to him. **deal** is here a verb in the infinitive mood. *Lord* is objective case after sees (179), and the order is: 'He sees no costly lord *to* deal the sumptuous banquet.'

182 **Vegetable meal,** a meal consisting of vegetable productions, such as rye, oat or barley bread, garlic, onions, beans, &c.

182 **Calm,** free from avarice and envy. This word qualifies *him* in the following line.

184 **Each wish contracting, fits him to the soil. Wish** here may be either nominative absolute (61) and **him** for himself (32), or *wish* may be nominative to *fits*, and *contracting* a neuter participle qualifying *wish*, which is the natural order in

32. Point out any passages in which Goldsmith has unjustly censured the French and make what additions seem necessary to complete description of their character

33 Make a list of leading French authors of Goldsmith's time and characterize their influence on subsequent European thought and action

34. Point out the particulars in which Goldsmith is [illegible]

4. [illegible] Dutch

[illegible] Refer to historical [illegible] of the bravery and patriotism of the Dutch

1 What are these lines upon
.. Line 302.

Tell what you know of
[illegible] [illegible] of [illegible]
[illegible] [illegible] [illegible] [illegible]
[illegible]

2 [illegible] lines which contain
allusions to the poet's personal
history

Examine relationship existing
between [illegible] [illegible] Dutch, English
Draw a diagram of the
[illegible] [illegible] [illegible] showing
easily how the English and
Dutch are related.

Cheerful at morn, he wakes from short repose,
Breathes the keen air, and carols as he goes;
With patient angle trolls the finny deep;
Or drives his vent'rous ploughshare to the steep;

the verse. Or again, *contracting* may be an active participle qualifying *he* understood and governing *wish* in the objective case, when the order will be: 'He, contracting each wish, fits himself to the soil.'

187 **Patient angle.** *Angle* is an O.E. word (*angul*) which formerly meant a hook, but became in time transferred to the fishing-rod.

> 'Give me mine *angle*,—we'll to the river.'
> Shakespeare, 'Antony and Cleopatra,' ii. 5.

In the same scene of this play, it is also used as a verb.

> 'Twas merry, when
> You wager'd on your *angling*.'—*ib.*

Chaucer uses the word *Angle-hook*, which shows that in his day the original meaning of the word was lost. The adj. *patient* is here transferred from the fisher to his rod. Cf. bleak (167). **trolls.** *To troll* (connected with *roll* and *drill*) is to move round and round either in the same or various places, and when this is done with the bait in fishing, it is called *trolling*. The word applies to the motion both of the angler and his reel. **finny.** *Fins* are those parts of fishes, like little wings, by which they balance themselves and swim through the water. The adj. *finny* is here transferred from the fish to the *deep*. Cf. (167–187). *Finny deep*, abounding in the finny tribe, i.e. in fish. It is, however, a rather forced construction. The following is better:—

> 'The breezy covers of the *warbling* grove,
> That only sheltered thefts of harmless love.'
> 'Deserted Village,' 361.

The poet could not very well have said the 'fishy deep,' nor could we speak of a 'horny' forest or a 'woolly' meadow.

183 **Vent'rous** for venturous; daring, bold, fearless. The adj. is here transferred from the driver of the plough, to the plough itself. Cf. finny (187). The meaning is that the peasant

Or seeks the den where snow-tracks mark the way,
And drags the struggling savage into day.
At night returning, every labour sped,
He sits him down the monarch of a shed ;
Smiles by his cheerful fire, and round surveys
His children's looks, that brighten at the blaze ;
While his loved partner, boastful of her hoard,
Displays her cleanly platter on the board :

drives his plough boldly to the edge of the steep precipice, heedless of danger. **ploughshare.** The *share* is the part of the plough with which the slice of earth is turned up after having been cut by the coulter. It is derived from the O. E. *sciran*, to cut or divide, whence we get also *sheer, sherd* (in pot*sherd*), *shred, shore, share, shire, short.*

190 **Savage**, any wild animal. The word originally meant an inhabitant of a forest or wood, from the Lat. *silva*, a wood, through the Fr. *sauvage*. The bear, wolf, fox, wild boar, stag, badger, marmot, otter, and chamois, are found in Switzerland. *Savage* is properly an adj., meaning wild, but is also used as a noun, by Conversion. Cf. *good* (26).

> 'Cornels and *savage* berries of the wood,
> And roots and herbs have been my meagre food.'
> Dryden, 'Trans. of the Æneid,' iii. 855.

In the following, the word alludes to the lion :

> 'When the grim *savage*, to his rifled den,
> Too late returning, snuffs the track of men.'
> Pope. 'Trans. of the Iliad.'

191 **Sped**, being sped or finished. This word is the passive participle of the verb *speed*, to despatch, hasten, execute.

192 **Shed**, a poor cottage. Hut is the nearest word in meaning to shed, but the homes of the Swiss peasantry are particularly neat and clean. **monarch** of a shed, i.e., he is as a king there, whatever he may be elsewhere. **sits him**, see note line 32.

195 **Hoard**, treasure, i.e., of plates and dishes, of which the female peasantry are often proud.

196 **Cleanly.** The young student will observe that this word,

Chronology [illegible], [illegible] .
of [illegible]

44 Describe the [illegible]tion
[illegible] the [illegible] Commis-
[illegible]

45 If [illegible] 535 [illegible]
[illegible] the [illegible] [illegible]
the rights [illegible]
[illegible] correct

6. Mention the [illegible]
which the [illegible] [illegible]
been [illegible]

7 [illegible]
[illegible] in England [illegible]
[illegible]
[illegible] in [illegible] 245 [illegible]

accompany the symptoms
of wealth upon the [illegible]
state according to the poet.
other writers have predicted
[illegible]
[illegible]
[illegible]
[illegible]
[illegible]
[illegible]
[illegible]
to which is now attached
the names of [illegible]
[illegible]
[illegible]
[illegible]

And haply too some pilgrim, thither led,
With many a tale repays the nightly bed.

Thus every good his native wilds impart
Imprints the patriot passion on his heart;
And e'en those ills, that round his mansion rise,
Enhance the bliss his scanty fund supplies,

when used as an adj. is pronounced short, *clenly*, but when used as an adv. it is pronounced long, *cleānly*. **Platter,** a large dish, generally of earthenware, but sometimes of metal or wood. **board,** table. *Board* is said to be derived from *broad* by the transposition of the letter r, as *shred* is derived from *sherd*, the participle of *shear* (O. E. *sciran*, to cut, 188), and as *throp* or *thrup* is derived from *thorpe*, a village. Cf. Hey*throp*, Bur*drop* = Bur*throp* = Bur*thorpe* (*Bur*, a knoll, a hill), Addles*trop*, Cracken*thorpe* (Crow village.) Cf. sprite 241.

197 **Haply,** perhaps, from *hap* = chance. **pilgrim,** (from the Lat. *peregrinus*, wandering, through the Italian *pelegrino*,) means any traveller or wanderer, especially for purposes of devotion.

198 **Nightly bed,** the bed granted for the night. A usual practice with hospitable nations, where inns are few and far between.

199 **Good,** after this word, the relative *which* must be supplied. *Good* is nom. to *imprints*. *Which* is obj. gov. by *impart*.

200 **Patriot,** a lover of his country, from the Lat. *patria*, one's own country, native land.

201 **Mansion** (167).

202 **Enhance,** to lift up, to raise on high; hence to heighten in price, raise in value, increase. Its original signification is seen in—

> 'Both of them high at once their hands *enhanc'd*,
> And both at once their huge blows down did sway.'
>
> Spenser, 'Faerie Queen.'

Fund, stock, capital, that by which any expense is supported, stock or bank of money. In the plural, *the funds*, it refers to that portion of the money lent to the Government of a country which cannot be withdrawn by the lenders. The word is derived from the Lat. *fundus*, a farm, through the French *fond*.

Dear is that shed to which his soul conforms,
And dear that hill which lifts him to the storms;
And as a child, when scaring sounds molest,
Clings close and closer to the mother's breast,
So the loud torrent, and the whirlwind's roar,
But bind him to his native mountains more.

Such are the charms to barren states assigned:
Their wants but few, their wishes all confined.
Yet let them only share the praises due,
If few their wants, their pleasures are but few;
For every want that stimulates the breast
Becomes a source of pleasure when redrest.

203 **Conforms.** This is an unusual use of the word, which is both active and neuter. As act. it is commonly used with the *reflective pronoun* and *to*.

'Then followed that most natural effect of *conforming one's self to* that which she did not like.'—Sir P. Sidney.

'Demand of them wherefore they *conform* not *themselves unto* the order of the Church.'—Hooker.

We use the verb in its neuter sense when we speak of conforming *to* the rules of a society, &c.

204 **Lifts him to the storms,** on account of its height. **Scaring,** frightening. **molest,** trouble, disturb. The word *him* must be understood after *molest*.

206 **Close and closer.** The usual phrase is *closer and closer*.

208 **But,** only.

209 **Such are the charms,** i.e. those the poet has enumerated, viz.: Contentment (175); cheerfulness (185); freedom (186); out-door employments, such as fishing (187), agriculture (188), hunting (189); independence (191); family pleasures (194); hospitality (197); patriotism (200). **barren states.** those that are less fertile than others. None are absolutely barren.

210 **Confined,** limited.

213 **Stimulates the breast,** i.e. excites it with a desire to supply the want, from Lat. *stimulus*, a goad.

214 **When redrest.** Redress is to set right, amend, relieve, remedy, ease; sometimes used of persons, but properly of things.

[illegible] — [illegible]
similar [illegible]

---

56. Examine the [illegible] made in lines [illegible]
57. What events of the time [illegible] suggested to the poet the [illegible] expressed in lines 381-5
58. Sketch the attempts of [illegible] to render [illegible] [illegible]
59. [illegible] from English [illegible] instances [illegible] [illegible]
60. [illegible] what [illegible] [illegible] to be the source of [illegible]
[illegible]

[illegible] the eye from a [illegible]
[illegible] and political [illegible]
[illegible] the part of the [illegible]
[illegible] which [illegible] the [illegible]
the [illegible]
[illegible]
[illegible]
[illegible]
[illegible]
[illegible] the [illegible]
[illegible] the times [illegible]
[illegible]
[illegible]

Hence from such lands each pleasing science flies,
That first excites desire, and then supplies;
Unknown to them, when sensual pleasures cloy,
To fill the languid pause with finer joy;

In the text, it is used in the same sense as in the following extract, which, however, is a rather unusual sense now: 'She felt with me what I felt of my captivity, and streight laboured to *redress* my pain, which was her pain.'—Sir P. Sidney.

215 **Hence,** i.e. from this cause, viz.: that their pleasures consist in the redressing of their ordinary wants. **Such lands,** i.e. the *barren states* mentioned in 209. **each pleasing science flies,** viz.:—Music, painting, sculpture, which are properly arts, not sciences. An *art* is that skill which is acquired by practice under certain rules. *Science* is properly the study of the various laws which govern the practice of an art. *Science* deals with principles, *art* with their application. Thus the study of the laws of harmony is a *science*, the practice of them on a musical instrument or with the voice is an *art*. A man may be proficient in the one, and yet know nothing of the other. The term *science* appears to be misapplied in the text.

'I present you with a man,
Cunning in music and the mathematicks,
To instruct her fully in those *sciences*.'
Shakespeare, 'Taming of the Shrew,' ii. 1.

Here *music* and *mathematics* may be considered as both arts and sciences.

216 **That,** rel. pron. referring to science. **first excites,** &c. The science, i.e. the knowledge of the delight to be derived from music, painting, &c. (215) excites the desire to enjoy it, and then supplies the means of doing so.

217 **Unknown to them,** &c. The construction is: '*How* to fill the languid pause with finer joy, when sensual pleasures cloy *them*, *is* unknown to them. *How* is often elegantly omitted after the verb to know, especially in Latin. **Sensual pleasures,** cf. 124, 213. **cloy,** is an active verb, and therefore must have *them* after it. It means to satiate, to fill up beyond desire. *Clod*, *clot*, *clog*, and *cloy*, are all connected, the original idea of them all being a thick, heavy, lump or mass. *Clown*, which conveys

Unknown those powers that raise the soul to flame,
Catch every nerve and vibrate through the frame.
Their level life is but a smouldering fire,
Nor quenched by want, nor fanned by strong desire ;
Unfit for raptures, or, if raptures cheer
On some high festival of once a year,
In wild excess the vulgar breast takes fire,
Till, buried in debauch, the bliss expire.

the idea of thickness and heaviness of intellect, is also related to them.

218 **The languid pause.** i.e. the period of weariness when the sensual pleasures, above alluded to, cease to give satisfaction, or when the body is too wearied to continue them. **finer joy.** The poet says above that *each pleasing science flies* from these lands, and, therefore, the people have no painting, sculpture, music, or learning to delight them when wearied with their *sensual pleasures.*

219 **Unknown,** &c. i.e. unknown *are* those powers. **that raise,** &c. *That* is nom. to *raise, catch,* and *vibrate.*

220 **To flame,** i.e. that stir up or excite the soul very greatly, as fine music, oratory, paintings, sculpture. &c. do.

221 **Their,** referring to the inhabitants of *barren states* (209). **level life,** even, tranquil, quiet life. **smouldering,** burning very slowly and without flame.

222 **Nor . . . nor** neither . . . nor.

223 **Raptures.** Violent feelings of pleasure when the soul is raised to flame (219). **cheer,** supply *them.* **vulgar,** belonging to the common people, from the Lat. *vulgus,* the common people. The word has now a further meaning, viz. :— rude, unbecoming, indecent, whilst its original one has become almost obsolete.

'Learn to say the Creed, the Lord's Prayer, and the Ten Commandments in the *Vulgar* tongue.'—'Book of Common Prayer, Exhortation at end of Office for Public Baptism of Infants.'

226 **Buried in debauch.** &c., i.e. they get so drunk that they lose all consciousness of pleasure, and of everything else. *Debauch,* a fit of intemperance, a term borrowed from the mason's craft. It is derived from *de,* and Old Fr. *bauche,* a row of bricks, and means literally a deviation from a straight line. **expire,** subjunctive for indicative *expires,* by poetical license.

[illegible]

What [illegible] of [illegible]

[illegible]

Who were the leaders [illegible]

[illegible]

[illegible]

How many [illegible]

[illegible]

[illegible] — 9

No other [illegible]

[illegible]

[illegible]

[illegible]

24. Make a list of [illegible]

[illegible], and particular [illegible]

[illegible]

[illegible] form a [illegible]

[illegible]

Here was the [illegible]

[illegible] developed [illegible]

[illegible]

[illegible] acknowledging them

[illegible] The [illegible]

[illegible] early

~~[illegible]~~ When was [illegible]

[illegible]

[illegible] beginning [illegible]

[illegible]

[illegible] the point [illegible]

But not their joys alone thus coarsely flow,—
Their morals, like their pleasures, are but low;
For, as refinement stops, from sire to son,
Unaltered, unimproved, the manners run;
And love's and friendship's finely-pointed dart
Fall, blunted, from each indurated heart.
Some sterner virtues o'er the mountain's breast
May sit, like falcons cowering on the nest;

227 The full sense is: 'But it is not their joys alone that thus coarsely flow.'

228 **Are but low**, i.e. are *only* low.

229 **As**, because. **from sire to son.** The construction is: 'Because refinement stops, the manners run, unalter'd and unimproved, from sire to son.'

231 'The finely pointed dart of love and friendship.'

232 **Fall blunted**: the more so because finely pointed at first. *Fall* should be *falls*. Probably the poet had in his mind the *dart* of *love* and the *dart* of *friendship* respectively; in fact, two darts, and hence he makes the verb agree with his meaning rather than the form of word he uses. This is called Synĕsis. **indurated,** hardened, rendered unfeeling, callous, from the Lat. *durus*, hard; *induro, induratum*, to make hard.

233 **Sterner virtues,** e.g. bravery, hardihood, love of freedom, &c.

234 **May sit.** In reading, stress must be laid upon *may*. The poet does not assert that they do; but he does assert that the gentler morals 'on timorous pinions fly.' **like** is an adjective, the only one in English that governs a case, which in O. E. was the dative, as in most languages which have inflections to a sufficient extent, e.g. the Latin. This is shown too, by the fact that if we use any preposition at all after *like* we use *to*, 'like *to* me,' 'like *to* death.' But as we have no dative case now in English, we say *like* governs the objective case. **Falcons.** The falcon is a bird of prey, so named from the shape of its bill, from the Lat. *falx, falcis*, a sickle. The best known species in the British Isles are the *Gyr Falcon*, the *Peregrine Falcon*, the *Hobby*, the *Merlin*, and the *Kestrel*. The *Peregrine Falcon* was formerly trained in this country to the pursuit of other birds. This sport was called *falconry*. **cowering**, a participle qualifying falcons. *To cower*

But all the gentler morals, such as play
Through life's more cultured walks, and charm the way,
These, far dispersed, on timorous pinions fly,
To sport and flutter in a kinder sky.

To kinder skies, where gentler manners reign,
I turn; and France displays her bright domain.

is to sink by bending the knees, to stoop; hence, to shrink. The idea appears to be that these 'sterner virtues' *cower* like falcons till something rouses them into activity.

235 **Gentler morals,** cultivation of the fine arts, politeness, &c.

236 **Charm the way,** beguile the tediousness and monotony of life's journey.

237 **These,** i.e. the gentler morals. It was necessary to use a second nominative for the sake of clearness, because of the parenthesis, 'such as play,' &c. The repetition of the nominative is a redundancy as regards grammar, but it is useful in rhetoric, for the purpose of emphasis. Cf. 'The Lord, *he* is the God; the Lord, *he* is the God,' 1 Kings xviii. 39. **timorous,** timid, fearful lest they should settle in an unfavourable spot. **pinions,** wings; derived from the Lat. *penna*, a feather, through the Norman-French *pignon*.

238 **Kinder,** more suited to their kind. *Kind* is derived from *kin*, relationship. A *kinned* or *kind* person is one who acknowledges and acts upon his *kinship* with other men.

> 'A little more than *kin* and less than *kind*.'
> Shakespeare, 'Hamlet.'

In the Church Litany, we pray that God will 'give and preserve to our use the *kindly* fruits of the earth,' i.e. the natural fruits; 'Each after its *kind*,' Gen. vii. 14. Sir Thomas More, in his 'Life of Richard III.' says, 'Richard thought by murdering his two nephews in the Tower of London to make himself a *kindly* king,' i.e. that he might be reckoned as king by his *kinship* to Edward IV.

239 **To kinder.** *Kinder* is here used in its present common signification; possibly also in the line above. **gentler.** Gentle is from the Lat. word *gens*, *gentis*, a family; and as every

[illegible]
[illegible] the chief [illegible]
[illegible] This [illegible]
[illegible] an account of Empire
[illegible]
[illegible] life
[illegible] the [illegible]
[illegible] affection [illegible]
[illegible]
[illegible]
[illegible]

Gay, sprightly land of mirth and social ease,
Pleased with thyself, whom all the world can please,
How often have I led thy sportive choir,
With tuneless pipe, beside the murmuring Loire!
Where shading elms along the margin grew,
And, freshened from the wave the zephyr flew;
And haply, though my harsh touch falt'ring still,
But mocked all tune, and marred the dancers' skill,
Yet would the village praise my wondrous power,
And dance, forgetful of th. noontide hour

well-born Roman was said to belong to a particular *gens*, of which he was more or less proud, the word came to mean pedigree, lineage, purity of blood, good birth, descent, breeding, good manners, and the like. It comes into our language through the French, and means well-born, though not noble, befitting a gentle man, soft, mild, peaceable, soothing.

241 **Sprightly** *spright* and *sprite* are different forms of *spirit*. For transposition of the r, cf. board 196.

242 **Whom all the world can please,** perhaps, in allusion to the politeness of the French people, which makes them appear pleased with everyone. His own success with his flute (247) demonstrates this. **led,** as a player on his flute during his wanderings. **sportive choir.** i.e. a merry band of dancers. The word choir comes from the Greek through the Lat. *chŏrus*, which means a dance in a ring, accompanied with a song.

244 **Tuneless.** The poet modestly hints that he was not a very proficient musician. **Loire,** the largest river of France. It flows into the Bay of Biscay.

246 **Freshen'd from the wave.** The air was made fresh and pure by passing over the water It is a well-known fact that water absorbs impurities from the air. **Zephyr** (173).

247 **Haply** (197). **harsh touch falt'ring,** i.e. he not only played *harshly*, but there was no certainty about his playing the right notes. **still** (9). See note (B) at the end.

248 **But,** only. **marr'd the dancers' skill,** i.e. he kept such bad time that the dancers could not keep with him without spoiling their dancing.

249 **The village.** The word is here put for the inhabitants

Alike all ages. Dames of ancient days
Have led their children through the mirthful maze,
And the gay grandsire, skilled in gestic lore,
Has frisked beneath the burthen of threescore.

of the village, by a figure of rhetoric called Metonymy. Cf. the phrase, 'the talk of *the place*.'

250 **Forgetful of the noontide hour,** forgetful that they were dancing in the hottest part of the day, or, perhaps, that it was dinner-time; probably, not that it was one of the hours of prayer. Noon now means midday. It is derived from the Latin *nona* (*hora*), the ninth hour, i.e. three o'clock in the afternoon, counting from six o'clock in the morning. In Norway, the word *non* or *nun* is still used in this sense to denote the third meal or resting time of the day. In Roman Catholic countries, e.g. France, Divine service was performed six times a day, viz.:—Matutina, prima, tertia, sexta, *nona*, vespera, completorium (now called *compline*). *Nona*, the fifth service, was held about midday in Italy at an early period. **tide** means time, and is seen in Whitsun*tide*, Shrove*tide*, &c.

251 **Alike all ages,** i.e. persons of all ages were alike fond of dancing to the sound of his pipe. **dame,** lady, mistress of a household. Fr. *dame*. Lat. *domina*.

252 **Mirthful maze,** of some dance like that known as 'Roger de Coverley.'

253 **Gestic,** relating to deeds of arms, &c, done by himself and others in the wars, or, perhaps, merely to dancing. The word comes from the Old French *geste* = an exploit, and this, from the Lat. *gero, gestum*, to carry on, to wage (war). Cf. jests, 19. **lore,** knowledge, learning

254 **Frisked,** danced, in spite of his age. **Thoughtless,** not without *thought*, in our present sense of the word, but without *anxiety*, which was its former meaning.

Cf. Our Saviour's words, 'Take no *thought* for your life, what ye shall eat, or what ye shall drink; nor yet for your body, what ye shall put on.'—St. Matt. vi. 25.

'He so plagued and vexed his father with injurious indignities, that the old man, for very *thought* and grief of heart, pined away and died.'—Holland, 'Camden's Ireland.'

'Harris, an Alderman of London, was put in trouble, and died

6. Who have written biographies of G.

7. What are the leading characteristics of the dramatic literature of this period

8. Trace the influence of the publication of Percy's Reliques upon poetical literature

9. Account for the failure of the rhyming couplet.

Name leading poems ...

... and ... prose ...

what ...

[illegible]

[illegible] humour

[illegible] the [illegible]

[illegible] from [illegible]

[illegible]

[illegible]

[illegible]

So a blest life these thoughtless realms display;
Thus idly busy rolls their world away:
Theirs are those arts that mind to mind endear,
For honour forms the social temper here;
Honour, that praise which real merit gains,
Or even imaginary worth obtains,
Here passes current; paid from hand to hand,
It shifts in splendid traffic round the land;

of *thought* and anxiety before his business came to an end.'—Bacon, 'History of Henry the Seventh.'

256 **Idly busy**, i.e. unprofitably employed, busy only in amusing themselves. This figure of rhetoric, where one word contradicts the other, is called Oxymoron. Cf. Lat. *festina lente*, make haste slowly, the motto and rebus of the *Onslow* family. **Rolls their world away.** As time passes, and we get nearer to eternity, the world may be said to roll away from us.

257 The order is: 'Theirs are those arts that endear mind to mind.' **arts**, i.e. of giving pleasure to others.

258 **Social temper**, the character and disposition of the people. The original meaning of the verb *to temper* is to mix things together, so that one part qualifies the other. The old physicians said there were four 'humours' in a man, viz.:—blood, choler, phlegm, and melancholy. When these were mixed or *tempered* in proper proportions, he was said to have an *even temper*. If choler predominated, he was said to be *choleric*, if phlegm, *phlegmatic*, and so on. We still speak of *tempering* mortar, i.e. mixing it properly. The noun *temper* was formerly used of the body as well as of the mind. 'The exquisiteness of the Saviour's bodily *temper* increased the exquisiteness of His torment.'—Fuller, 'A Pisgah Sight of Palestine.' **Here**, i.e. in France (240).

259 **Honour**, nominative to passes (261). **praise**, in opposition to honour. These lines contain a very good definition of the word. Honour is derived from the Lat. *honor*, through the French *honneur*, which accounts for the u.

261 **Passes current**, an allusion to money, which is said to be *current* when it is commonly received and passes from one to another. *Current* is derived from the Lat. *curro*, *cursum*, to run, and is here an adj., used adverbially. Neuter verbs (e.g. passes)

From courts to camps, to cottages it strays,
And all are taught an avarice of praise :
They please, are pleased, they give to get esteem,
Till, seeming blest, they grow to what they seem.

But while this softer art their bliss supplies,
It gives their follies also room to rise;

are frequently followed by adjectives, instead of adverbs, as, *the stars shine bright; the time flies fast; he hits hard, he shuts the door close.*

'How *sweet* the moonlight sleeps upon this bank!'
Shakespeare.

This may be due to the fact that in O. E. the adv. was often formed from the adj. by adding e, (thus, adj. soft, adv. softe), which, in course of time, like many other endings, was dropped ; or to the fact that, in many cases, the adj. form is intended to express rather the quality of the agent as seen in the act, or after the act, than the quality of the act i. e f.

262 **Shifts**, moves. **traffic.** This word is said to come to us through the Fr. *trafique*, from the Lat. *trans*, across, and *fretum*, sea. Others say it is from the Italian *trafficare*, Lat. *trans*, across, and *facere*, to do, i.e. to carry on business beyond sea. *Traffic* originally referred to foreign commerce, whilst *trade* referred to that carried on in the country. It is now used of trading generally, but has acquired the wider signification of 'passing to and fro,' as when we speak of the *traffic* in the streets. *Splendid traffic*, alludes to the wealth which commerce brings, and the magnificence with which it is accompanied.

263 **From courts to camps.** Kings and courtiers and soldiers.

264 **Avarice of praise**, an eager desire for it.

265 **They give to get esteem,** i.e. they give esteem in order that they may get esteem; they honour others, that they themselves may be honoured in return.

266 **Grow to what they seem.** They get the credit for being worthy of honour, and, being anxious to retain it, are so careful of their conduct, that they become really worthy of it. So, the surest way to make a man a liar or a thief is to treat him as one.

Thomson

Poets. Gray

Pope.

Cibber

Richardson.

175

[illegible]

[illegible] was in way [illegible] showing [illegible] with any sense of presence of nature. he [illegible]

[illegible] 1790,

[illegible]

For praise too dearly loved, or warmly sought,
Enfeebles all internal strength of thought:
And the weak soul, within itself unblest,
Leans for all pleasure on another's breast.
Hence ostentation here, with tawdry art,
Pants for the vulgar praise which fools impart;

267 **Softer,** more pleasing. **art,** the art of pleasing.

270 **Enfeebles.** Praise, too dearly loved, or sought too eagerly, leads men to do what will meet the approval of men rather than what is absolutely right.

272 **On another's breast,** i.e. craves, as its greatest happiness, the praise of others instead of an approving conscience.

273 **Hence,** i.e. for the reasons just given. **Ostentation** is here spoken of as a person, and is said to be personified by a figure of speech called Prosopopœia or Personification. This is very frequent in the poetry of the 18th century. *Ostentation* now means ambitious display, boast, vain show; but formerly, outward show or appearance.

'You are come
A market-maid to Rome, and have prevented
The *ostentation* of our love.'
Shakespeare, 'Antony and Cleopatra,' iii. 6.

here, in France. **tawdry,** meanly fine, shabbily splendid. This word is a corruption of St. Audry, a familiar name of the founder and first abbess of Ely (O.E. Œthelthryth, Lat. form Œtheldreda). The Cathedral of this city, being built on the site of the ancient convent, is dedicated to St. Audry and St. Peter. 'At the fair of St. Audry at Ely in former times toys of all sorts were sold and a description of cheap necklaces, which, under the name of "tawdry laces," long enjoyed great celebrity. Various allusions to *tawdry laces* occur in Shakespeare, Spenser, and other writers of their age.' —Chambers, 'Book of Days.'

'Not the smallest beck,
But with white pebbles makes her *tawdries* for her neck.'
Drayton, 'Polyolbion.'

A *beck* is a small stream.

275 **Pert,** sprightly, bold. This word is now commonly used in a bad sense, meaning impudent, for which *malapert* was for-

Here vanity assumes her pert grimace,
And trims her robes of frieze with copper lace;
Here beggar pride defrauds her daily cheer,
To boast one splendid banquet once a year:

merly employed, and *pert* meant spirited, lively, brisk (probably connected with *pretty*).

> 'Awake the *pert* and nimble spirit of mirth;
> Turn melancholy forth to funerals.'
>
> Shakespeare, 'Mids. N. D.' i. 1.

> 'On the tawny sands and shelves,
> Trip the *pert* fairies and the dapper elves.'
>
> Milton, 'Comus.'

Grimace, a pure French word, which has become so completely anglicised that it has lost its original pronunciation. It means a distortion of the face from habit, affectation, or insolence. There is an old Scandinavian word *grima*, meaning a mask. 'The French nation is addicted to *grimace*.'—'The Spectator.'

276 **Frieze.** A kind of coarse woollen cloth, much worn in Ireland. This word is commonly, in England, mispronounced to rhyme with *freeze*. But cf.

> 'The captive Germans of gigantic *size*
> Are rank'd in order, and are clad in *frieze*.'
>
> Dryden, 'Translation of Persius.'

> 'See how the double nation *lies*,
> Like a rich coat with skirts of *frieze*;
> As if a man in making posies,
> Should bundle thistles up with roses.' Swift.

Swift was an Irishman, who ought to know.

276 **Copper lace.** Gold or silver lace adorned the dress of persons of fashion at that time. Those of whom the poet speaks used an imitation made of *copper*.

277 **Beggar pride**, or, as we should say, *beggarly pride*, *beggar* being rarely employed as an adj. **pride**, an example of personification (273). **defrauds**, i.e. lives very sparingly the rest of the year in order to have one grand feast before its close. **cheer**, supply of food. Thus we speak of a table laden with good

the [illegible] poems [illegible]
in this
6. Distinguish essay & paragraph
7. Sketch the history of the [illegible]
of the elegy
8. Quote a [illegible] from [illegible]
[illegible]
9. [illegible] the [illegible]
[illegible] of the [illegible]

[illegible] The [illegible]

[illegible] meaning of the [illegible]

[illegible]

[illegible] the [illegible]

[illegible]

[illegible] amount [illegible]

[illegible]

[illegible] per [illegible]

[illegible] lea, landscape [illegible]

[illegible] amount [illegible]

[illegible]

The mind still turns where shifting fashion draws,
Nor weighs the solid worth of self-applause.

To men of other minds my fancy flies,
Embosomed in the deep where Holland lies.
Methinks her patient sons before me stand,
Where the broad ocean leans against the land ;
And, sedulous to stop the coming tide,
Lift the tall rampire's artificial pride.

cheer. It is derived from an old French word *chière*, countenance, and was formerly used for face, visage, a sense in which it is now obsolete.

'So that the children of Israel might not biholde into the face of Moises for the glory of his *cheer.*' Wycliffe, 'Trans. of New Test.' 2 Cor. iii. 7.

280 **Nor weighs**, i.e. and does not consider how much better the approval of one's own conscience is than the applause of others.

282 **Holland**, i.e. hollow-land, the greater part of the country being below the level of the sea, from the inroads of which it is protected by dykes. This fact, and a reference to the map of Europe, will show the appropriateness of the expression **embosom'd in the deep.** A part of Lincolnshire, similar in character to the country alluded to, is also called Holland.

283 **Methinks**, it seems to me, it appears to me. In this word, *me* is a dative form, and thinks is from the O.E. *thincan*, to seem, to appear. *Thencan*, to think, was a different word.

'It *thinketh me* I sing as well as thou.' Chaucer.

284 **Leans against the wall**, i.e. is higher than the level of the land (282), and therefore may be said to *lean against* the natural sand-banks and artificial dykes which surround it on the sea-board.

285 **Sedulous to stop.** Sedulous (Lat. *sedulus*) means assiduous, industrious, laborious, persevering, diligent. This character of the Dutch is well evinced by their present plan (1876) of recovering the Zuyder Zee, which was formerly a fertile and populous plain, but was overflowed by the sea in 1421, when seventy-two villages and towns were destroyed, and 100,000 people perished.

Onward, methinks, and diligently slow,
The firm connected bulwark seems to grow,
Spreads its long arms amidst the watery roar,
Scoops out an empire, and usurps the shore :
While the pent ocean, rising o'er the pile,
Sees an amphibious world beneath him smile ;

They purpose to do this by building huge dykes and pumping out the water, as they have already done with respect to the Lake of Haarlem. They will thus recover about 2,000 square miles of territory.

286 **Tall rampire's artificial pride.** A *rampire* is a rampart or wall to fortify a place. This word is seldom employed except in poetry. *Artificial* is used to distinguish it from the *natural* rampart, consisting of downs or sandbanks, sometimes 180 feet high, which protect the coast in several parts.

287 **Methinks** (283), **diligently slow**, i.e. they are careful to allow the work time to settle as they progress, otherwise it might prove unequal to the pressure of the sea against it. Lamentable accidents have sometimes occurred from 'running up' the walls of houses too rapidly. An example of Oxymoron, cf. 256.

288 **Bulwark** (derived from a Dutch word *bol*, meaning the trunk of a tree, and *werck*,) means a bastion, fortification, security, screen, shelter.

290 **Scoops out an empire.** There is some poetical exaggeration here, though the Dutch have rescued large tracts of land from the sea. The case is analogous to that of the River Thames at London, where a large quantity of land has been thus rescued by means of the Thames Embankments. **usurps**, takes possession of (Lat. *usurpo*; Fr. *usurper*). **Shore**, the space of land between high-water mark and low-water mark.

291 **Pent**, the past participle of the verb *to pen*, to coop, shut up, confine in a narrow place, used adjectively. It is from the O.E. *pyndan*, whence also *pound*, a place where cattle found straying are confined, *pond*, a place where water is confined, and *pen*, for sheep, are derived. *Pen*, an instrument for writing with, is derived from the Lat. *penna*, a feather. The ocean is *pent*, i.e. restrained by the 'firm connected bulwark' (288). **rising o'er the pile.** The sea sometimes presents this appearance in

18. how many editions

[illegible]

17. [illegible]

[illegible]

19. Give a table of

[illegible]

[illegible]

1. [illegible] not on building

[illegible]

[illegible]

[illegible]

[illegible]

[illegible]

3. [illegible] [illegible] Th[illegible]

[illegible]

4. What [illegible]

[illegible]

[illegible]

The slow canal, the yellow blossomed vale,
The willow-tufted bank, the gliding sail,
The crowded mart, the cultivated plain,
A new creation rescued from his reign.

Thus, while around the wave-subjected soil
Impels the native to repeated toil,

Holland, so that persons in the low lands, looking up, see ships passing above them in the canals and near the coast.

292 **Amphibious**, from two Greek words *amphi*, both, and *bios*, life, means, strictly, able to live both in water and in air. The Dutch, of course, cannot do this, but they live a great deal *upon* the water; canals in many parts of the country taking the place of streets, and boats being used where we should use various kinds of wheeled carriages. This is also the case in Venice. **smile**, verb inf. *to smile*. The Dutch, in spite of their many disadvantages, are a very industrious, prosperous, and happy people.

293 **Canal**, Latin *canalis*, a water-pipe, from *canna*, a reed. **yellow-blossom'd vale**. A great portion of the soil of Holland is of a marshy nature, very suited to pasturage, and here plants of the 'buttercup' kind with yellow blossoms abound.

294 **Willow-tufted bank**. In Holland, the dykes and margins of the canals are usually planted with willows, which, being frequently lopped for the sake of their long, straight and pliable branches, as in England, present a tufted appearance.

295 **The crowded mart**. Holland at this time held a foremost place in the commerce of the world. The spices and precious stones of the East passed through her hands. *Mart* is the same as *market*. Fr. *marché*. Lat. *merx*, merchandise. **cultivated plain**. Holland is cultivated like a garden, and supports, for its size, an immense population.

296 **Creation**. This word is in apposition to *world* (292), *canal*, *vale* (293), *bank*, *sail* (294), *mart and plain* (295), all of which are in the obj. case after sees (291). **his**, i.e. Ocean's (291).

297 **Wave-subjected soil**, the land constantly *subjected* to the overflowing of the sea, which frequently takes place and thus 'impels the natives to repeated toil' in keeping their dams and dykes in good order, in rebuilding them, and in pumping out the water whenever an inundation occurs.

Industrious habits in each bosom reign,
And industry begets a love of gain.
Hence all the good from opulence that springs,
With all those ills superfluous treasure brings,
Are here displayed. Their much-loved wealth imparts
Convenience, plenty, elegance, and arts;
But view them closer, craft and fraud appear,
Even liberty itself is bartered here.
At gold's superior charms all freedom flies;
The needy sell it, and the rich man buys:
A land of tyrants, and a den of slaves,
Here wretches seek dishonourable graves,
And, calmly bent, to servitude conform,
Dull as their lakes that slumber in the storm.

301 **Hence,** &c. The order is: 'All the good that springs from opulence.' **good** = good things (26). **opulence,** wealth.

303 **Are.** The nom. to this verb is 'all the *good* with all those *ills*,' where *with* = and. The plural form *goods* has a somewhat different meaning (26).

305 **Craft,** dishonest trickery. Not always with this meaning. Cf. *craftsman*, handi*craft*.

305-6 These lines refer to the political struggles which long disturbed the Netherlands. The Republican party received assistance from France, to the amount of more than a million of money, and though the House of Orange triumphed in 1747, it held its sway with difficulty.

308 **It,** i.e. freedom.

309 This line occurs in Goldsmith's 'Chinese Letters, or Citizen of the World.' 'Into what state of misery are the Western Persians fallen! A nation once famous for setting the world an example of freedom is now become *a land of tyrants and a den of slaves.*'

311 **Calmly bent,** disposed for peace at any price. **conform** (203). The nom. to this verb is *wretches* (310).

312 **Dull.** The Dutch have the character of being slow, heavy and phlegmatic **slumber in the storm,** i.e. owing to their shallowness and comparatively small size, they are not much affected by winds.

[illegible]

[illegible]

[illegible]

[illegible]

[illegible]

[illegible]

[illegible]

[illegible]

[illegible]

[illegible]

Heavens! how unlike their Belgic sires of old!
Rough, poor, content, ungovernably bold,
War in each breast, and freedom on each brow,
How much unlike the sons of Britain now!

Fired at the sound, my genius spreads her wing,
And flies where Britain courts the western spring;

313 **Unlike,** an adj. governing obj. case. Cf. like (234). **Belgic sires.** The tribes who inhabited this region in Roman times were known as *Belgæ*, and were famous for their sturdy resistance to the Roman arms under Julius Cæsar. Their name still survives in that of Belgium. **sire** is an old French word, meaning an elder, from Lat. *senior*, compar. of *senex*, old. It commonly means father or ancestor with us, and is always used as a title of respect, especially in addressing a king. Our common word *sir* is an abbreviation of *sire*.

316 **Sons of Britain.** The poet compares the descendants of the Belgæ with those of the Ancient Britons, because the latter, who were Gauls or Celts, were similar in character to the Belgæ. The present 'sons of Britain' are, however, rather Saxon than Celtic, though some of the latter race are found among the Highlanders of Scotland, and in Wales.

317 **My genius,** &c. According to old classical fables it was supposed that every person is attended in life by one or more spirits called genii (plu. of *genius*), who are the advisers of those whom they attend. When *genius* denotes mental abilities, or a person eminently possessed of these, the plural is *geniuses*. *Genius* in the text, however, is used instead of Muse, the genius of poetry, whom poets frequently invoke. Hence he uses the pronoun **her,** muse (Lat. *musa*) being feminine, whilst *genius* is masculine.

318 **Britain courts the western spring.** The poet probably means no more than that Britain is favourably situated for receiving the benefit of the warm winds blowing from the west, which cause the spring of the year to be earlier here than in the countries on the Continent of Europe. This is, of course, even more applicable to Ireland, which, however, is not included under the name Britain. Cf. 'The Deserted Village,' 3, 4.:

> 'While *smiling spring its earliest visit paid,*
> And parting summer's lingering blooms delay'd.'

Where lawns extend that scorn Arcadian pride,
And brighter streams than famed Hydaspes glide.
There, all around, the gentlest breezes stray;
There gentle music melts on ev'ry spray;

319 **Lawns** *Lawn*, originally *land*, or *laund* now means a stretch of smooth grass in front of a house Goldsmith uses it in 'The Deserted Village (35) to express a wide tract of country containing several villages, and calls Auburn the loveliest of them all:

> 'Sweet smiling village, loveliest of the *lawn*.'

Milton also uses it in its original sense—

> 'Russet *lawns* and fallows gray,
> Where the nibbling flocks do stray'
>
> 'L'Allegro.'

> 'Betwixt them *lawns* or level downs, and flocks,
> Grazing the tender herb, were interpos'd.'
>
> 'Paradise Lost.'

In the text the word signifies large stretches of pasture land. *Lawn*, fine linen, is another word entirely, being derived from the Lat. *lana*, wool **Arcadian** Arcadia was one of the inland divisions of that part of Ancient Greece which is now called the Morea. From its beautiful vales and the simple habits of its people, ancient and modern poets have sung its praises as the model land of peace, innocence, pastoral beauty, and simplicity. **Pride**, fame, glory. Goldsmith frequently uses this word in a good sense.

320 **Hydaspes.** A river of India, now called the Jelum, which rises in the Himalayas and flows through the Punjaub into the Indus It was the Eastern boundary of the conquests of Alexander the Great. Horace, a celebrated Latin poet, writes of this river as 'fabulosus Hydaspes,' i.e. Hydaspes, celebrated in story, because many wonderful things were related about it. (Odes, i. 22. 7.)

321 **There**, i.e. in *Britain*. England is properly *Britain*. England and Scotland form *Great Britain*. When Ireland is included, the term *Great Britain and Ireland* is used. **All around.** Both these words are adverbs here, the first qualifying the second.

322 **Gentle music melts**, &c. In allusion to the sweet songs of the birds, e.g. the nightingale, thrush, blackbird, bullfinch, &c. *Melt* is here a neuter verb, to grow tender, mild, or gentle,

[illegible]

[illegible]

55 [illegible]

[illegible]

[illegible]

115 [illegible]

[illegible]

---

6 [illegible]

[illegible] 117, 118

[illegible]

[illegible]

[illegible]

[illegible]

Dr Johnson [illegible]

[illegible]

Creation's mildest charms are there combined :
Extremes are only in the master's mind.
Stern o'er each bosom Reason holds her state,
With daring aims irregularly great.

and well characterizes the notes of our best feathered songsters. Cf.

> 'The strains decay and *melt* away,
> In a dying, dying fall.'
>
> Pope, 'Ode on St Cecilia's Day.'

323 **Mildest charms**, i e. there are no such mountains as the Alps no such forests as those of Italy, no volcanoes, no such rivers as the Amazon and Mississippi or even as the Loire. The natural beauties of England are all on a smaller scale, and are therefore without that grandeur which other countries possess.

324 **In the master's mind**. This line is somewhat obscure, but the meaning appears to be that the only extremes to be found in Britain are in the minds of the natives of the country. These extremes he describes (344–348) as minds combating minds, ferments, factions and ambition struggling round her shore. The meaning of the line will be more clear if *master's* be changed to *masters*.

325 **Reason holds her state**, holds her sway. i e. reason is mistress of their thoughts and actions; in contrast with the character of the French nation (266–270).

326 **With daring aims irregularly great**. This line is somewhat obscure; for the adj. *great* may qualify *reason*, *state*, or *aims* But whichever it be, the meaning probably is that some of the objects aimed at are great on account of the benefits they will confer on the nation and individuals, whilst others are great on account of their injustice. It may, however, simply mean that some aims are greater than others. But the word *daring* inclines one to the former interpretation.

327 **Port** the manner in which a person bears himself; his demeanour. The word comes from the Lat. *porto*, to carry through; the French *porter*. Cf.

> 'Her lion *port*, her awe-commanding face.'
>
> Gray, 'The Bard.'
>
> 'Like a modern gentleman of stateliest *port*.'
>
> Tennyson.

Pride in their port, defiance in their eye,
I see the lords of human kind pass by,
Intent on high designs, a thoughtful band,
By forms unfashioned, fresh from nature's hand,
Fierce in their native hardiness of soul,
True to imagined right, above control;

Port, a gate (Lat. *porta*), is said to derive its name from the fact that when the boundary of Rome was first marked out with the plough the latter was *carried* (Lat. *porto*, to carry), so as to make no furrow at those points where gates were to be placed. *Port*, a kind of wine, derives its name from *Oporto*. A *porter* is a carrier of burthens for hire; and *porter*, a kind of strong beer, is so called because much drunk by *porters*. In this last sense it came into use about 1750. **Defiance**, a challenge, expression of hatred or contempt, from the verb *defy*. This word is derived from the Lat. *de*, from, and *fides*, faith, through the Norman-French *défier*. Originally it meant to declare all bonds of faith and friendship between the defier and defied to be entirely set aside, so that nothing should prevent the greatest hostility between them. When one sent a *defiance* to another, he did not by that word proclaim war, but simply declared that all kind feeling between them was at an end, and thus it came to mean *to disclaim* or *renounce*.

'All studies here I solemnly *defy*,
Save how to gall and pinch this Bolingbroke.'
Shakespeare, '1 Henry iv.' i. 3.

'No man, speaking in the Spirit of God, *defieth* Jesus Christ.'
Tyndall, Trans. of N. T. 1 Cor. xii. 3.

328 **Lords of human kind**, alluding to the supremacy of the English (Sons of Britain, 316) in war, arts, commerce, &c. They had recently had many successes in war against the Spaniards and French as well as in India, but had not yet been subjected to those reverses which led to the declaration of American Independence in 1776.

330 **By forms unfashioned**, i.e. not polished like the French people, of whom the poet says (257)

'Theirs are those arts that mind to mind endear.'

[illegible]

what [illegible]
[illegible]
[illegible] are [illegible]
[illegible] for the [illegible]

What was [illegible]
[illegible] was [illegible]

[illegible]
[illegible]
[illegible]

While e'en the peasant boasts these rights to scan,
And learns to venerate himself as man.

Thine, Freedom, thine the blessings pictured here,
Thine are those charms that dazzle and endear;
Too blest, indeed, were such without alloy,
But fostered e'en by freedom, ills annoy;

332 **True to imagined right**, i.e. holding firmly to what they consider to be justice, and maintaining their rights.

333 **Peasant** (83). **Scan**, examines carefully, not only his own rights, but also those which others claim; and boasts that he has the right to do so. Scan is literally to climb: Fr. *scander*; Lat. *scando*. Hence to count the feet in a verse, to examine carefully.

334 **To venerate himself as man**, to respect himself, which his class could scarcely do when they were bought and sold with the land. Domesday book shows that the toll at Lewes Market was a penny for a cow and fourpence for a slave. The Anglo-Saxons exported many British slaves to Ireland, where they fetched high prices. Serfdom in England had practically died out soon after the time of Richard II., and was abolished by law in the reign of Queen Elizabeth, but it existed to some extent in Scotland till that of George III. Till then the colliers and salters were bought and sold with the soil. Cf. note C., at end. Perhaps the poet had in his mind the serfs of Russia and the negro slaves of America, for 'slaves breathed in England' down to 1806, when the Bill for the Abolition of the Slave Trade was carried. These last ten lines are said to have been so admired by Dr. Johnson that he never repeated them without shedding tears.

336 **Dazzle**, to blind the eyes with an excess of light, so as to prevent their seeing distinctly the evils of freedom.

337 **Were**, subjunctive mood = would be, i.e. such blessings and charms *would be* too blest if they had no alloy. **Alloy** is from the French *à loi* = according to law. It means a base metal, such as copper, tin, iron, &c., which is mixed with gold or silver for the coinage of money, the precious metals being too soft to be used alone. The proportion of baser metal permitted was fixed by law, *à loi*, hence the word is used to signify any inferior thing mixed with a better.

That independence Britons prize too high,
Keeps man from man, and breaks the social tie :
The self-dependent lordlings stand alone,
All claims that bind and sweeten life unknown.
Here, by the bonds of nature feebly held,
Minds combat minds, repelling and repelled ;
Ferments arise, imprisoned factions roar,
Represt ambition struggles round her shore,

338 The order is : 'But ills, fostered even by freedom, annoy.

339 Supply the relative *which* after independence. *That* is demonstrative. **High**, adj., for adv. highly.

340 **Keeps man from man.** Each, considering himself independent of the other, takes no trouble to please him, and consequently there is an absence of those kindly feelings between them which the giving and receiving of pleasure promotes.

341 **Lordlings**, little lords ; contemptuously, 'a bit of a lord.' *Ling* is an O.E. diminutive, which expresses in itself nothing of contempt. Thus we have *darling*, a little dear ; *gosling*, a little goose ; *duckling*, a little duck, &c. *Lordling* was also once used without any notion of disparagement. In the text, however, the poet speaks of Englishmen generally as 'self-dependent lordlings,' i.e. as boastfully independent of others as any lord might claim to be.

342 **All claims**, &c. This is, of course, poetical exaggeration.

343 **By the bonds of nature feebly held**, i.e. a man does not mind whether he whom he opposes be his father, brother, fellow-countryman, &c., or not.

344 **Minds combat minds** in the struggle for political power.

345 **Ferments arise,** i.e., disturbances, riots, &c., take place, probably in allusion to those on account of the prosecution of Wilkes for articles reflecting on the Government of the day in the *North Briton* (1763).

346 **Represt** = repressed, which is the usual prose form of the word. It here means *which was at one time repressed.* **Ambition**, a desire of honour or power ; from the Latin *ambi*, about, and *eo*, *itum*, to go. The word *ambitio* meant originally

Till, overwrought, the general system feels
Its motions stop, or frenzy fire the wheels.

Nor this the worst. As nature's ties decay,
As duty, love, and honour fail to sway,
Fictitious bonds, the bonds of wealth and law,
Still gather strength, and force unwilling awe.
Hence all obedience bows to these alone,
And talent sinks, and merit weeps unknown;
Till time may come, when, stripped of all her charms,
The land of scholars, and the nurse of arms,

among the Romans a going up and down the city asking for votes. Those who did this were clad in white or distinguished by some white article of dress, and were hence called *candidati* (Lat. *candidus*, white), from which our word *candidate* is derived.

347 **System.** Society as a whole, political as well as social.

348 **Stop**, infinitive = *to* stop. **frenzy**, madness, or excitement of the mind approaching to it. **fire**, infinitive = *to* fire, i.e. to set on fire. **wheels**, in allusion to the fact that when a carriage runs very fast the wood-work near the axle is liable to be set on fire by friction unless the parts are properly lubricated with grease. As the whole carriage is thus liable to be destroyed, so the 'general system' of society is likely to be destroyed by the ferments, factions, &c., alluded to.

349 **Nor this**, &c. Supply *is*.

350 **To sway**, to influence men's actions.

351 **Fictitious bonds**, artificial bonds, in opposition to *nature's ties* (349).

352 **Force unwilling awe**, compel men against their will to pay respect to them.

353 **These**, i.e. the bonds of wealth and law.

354 **Talent and merit** are here personified, or they may be considered as abstract nouns used for concrete, i.e. for persons of talent and merit. Where *wealth* has too great influence, and *law* is enforced apart from equity, talent and merit are equally slighted.

355 **Till time**, i.e. till *the* time.

356 **Land of scholars**, i.e. England, famed for men of learning. **Nurse of arms**, who has nurtured men famous in war.

Where noble stems transmit the patriot flame,
Where kings have toiled, and poets wrote for fame,
One sink of level avarice shall lie,
And scholars, soldiers, kings, unhonoured die.

Yet think not, thus when freedom's ills I state,
I mean to flatter kings, or court the great.
Ye powers of truth, that bid my soul aspire,
Far from my bosom drive the low desire !
And thou, fair freedom, taught alike to feel
The rabble's rage, and tyrant's angry steel ;
Thou transitory flower, alike undone
By proud contempt, or favour's fostering sun,

357 **Noble stems**, i.e. fathers famous as scholars or as warriors transmit their noble qualities to their children. **Patriot**, as an adj., means relating to the love of one's country (Lat. *patria*, one's own country, fatherland).

358 **Have toiled**, i.e. for fame. **Poets wrote for fame**, not for bread, as Goldsmith hints they did in his day. *Wrote* is here for *have written*.

359 **One sink**. A sink is a place provided for dirty water to *sink* away. The meaning is that the land shall become the receptacle of all the vices arising from national avarice, and that all the people shall be alike brought to a low level as regards learning, bravery, and virtue. **Shall lie**, the nominatives to this verb are *land* and *nurse* (356).

360 **Unhonoured**, i.e. they shall receive no honour because the people will be too debased to appreciate them. We scarcely need say that the poet's forebodings have not yet been realised in England.

363 **Powers of truth**, nom. of address.

364 **Drive**, imperative. **Low desire**, i.e. of flattering kings or courting great personages.

366 **Rabble**, a noisy crowd, probably from Lat. *rabula*, a noisy lawyer, connected with *rabies*, madness, *rabo*, to be mad. **Tyrant's angry steel.** The cause of freedom has frequently suffered from the rage of an unreasonable rabble, as well as from the sword or execution axe of tyrannical sovereigns.

Still may thy blooms the changeful clime endure!
I only would repress them to secure.
For just experience tells, in ev'ry soil,
That those who think must govern those that toil;
And all that freedom's highest aims can reach
Is but to lay proportioned loads on each.
Hence, should one order disproportioned grow,
Its double weight must ruin all below.

O, then, how blind to all that truth requires,
Who think it freedom when a part aspires!

367 **Transitory**, fading quickly, passing away. **Flower**, nominative of address in apposition to freedom (365). **alike undone**, ruined equally by contempt or favour (368).

369. **Still may**, &c. The sense is, 'May the blooms of freedom,' viz., the blessings referred to in line 335, 'endure the injurious influences' of 'proud contempt, or favour's fostering sun,' which are alluded to in the expression 'changeful clime.'

370 **Repress them**, keep them in check. Supply *them* after secure. The meaning of the line is, 'I would keep the blooms of the transitory flower, Freedom, in check only to preserve them safe, lest, growing too fast in a changeful climate, they may be injured by cold or heat, rain or drought.'

371 **Tells**, teaches. **Every soil**, i.e. in every country where the 'transitory flower, Freedom,' grows at all.

372 **Those that think**, &c. Reason teaches this too, but the argument drawn from experience is even greater. Those who toil at manual labour have, as a rule, neither the time nor the learning requisite for the study of political or social economy.

374 **Proportioned loads on each**, i.e. that both thinkers and toilers should have their due burdens in the state—no more and no less.

375 **One order disproportioned**, &c., i.e. if the order or class of thinkers should be too numerous and powerful, it would oppress and ruin the toiling class, and *vice versâ*.

377 **How blind**, i.e. how blind *are they*, &c.

378 **A part**. The poet is here censuring those who think that freedom means the elevation of the 'toilers' to more than their

Calm is my soul, nor apt to rise in arms,
Except when fast approaching danger warms ;
But, when contending chiefs blockade the throne,
Contracting regal power to stretch their own,
When I behold a factious band agree
To call it freedom when themselves are free ;

fair share of power and influence in the country. Freedom is a thing that all must share. **Aspires,** rises, soars, so Waller writes :

> My own breath still foments the fire,
> Which flames as high as fancy can *aspire.*'

379 **Nor,** and not.

380 **Warms,** excites, *it* understood, ref. to soul. Earlier editions have warns. Arms and warms must certainly be considered a defective rhyme to southern ears, though in many parts of the north of England these two words, according to the pronunciation of the people, would form a perfect one.

381 **Blockade the throne,** make it inaccessible to the complaints of the poor. It is uncertain whether Goldsmith alludes to any historical personages of his own time here ; but, in the Preface to his 'History of England,' he writes : 'For my own part, from seeing the bad effects of the tyranny of the great in those Republican States that pretend to be free, I cannot help wishing that our monarchs may still be allowed to enjoy the power of controlling the encroachments of the great at home.'

383 **Factious band,** a number of persons banded together for the personal interests of its members and leaders as opposed to those of the State.

384 Supply *they* before **themselves.** The compounds of *self* are very irregular. In *my-self, thy-self, your-self, our-selves, your-selves,* self is a common substantive compounded with an adjective, *my, thy, our, your,* which may also be considered as possessive pronouns. In *him-self, them-selves,* when in the objective case, the noun *self, selves* is in apposition to *him, them.* When used in the nom. case, however, *he himself, they themselves,* there is no apposition between *him* and *self, them* and *selves,* but *himself* and *themselves* must be considered as simple words compounded. *Herself* is ambiguous, since *her* is both possessive and

Each wanton judge new penal statutes draw,
Laws grind the poor, and rich men rule the law ;
The wealth of climes, where savage nations roam
Pillaged from slaves to purchase slaves at home ;
Fear, pity, justice, indignation start,
Tear off reserve, and bare my swelling heart ;

objective case. *Itself* is also ambiguous, since the s may be a part either of *its* or of *self*. The irregularities and inconsistencies of this word are as old as the English language. All the forms are used for the purpose of emphasis.

385 **Wanton**, unrestrained, unchecked. So writes Addison :

'How does your tongue grow *wanton* in her praise !'

The word is compounded of the O.E. *wan* (allied to *want* and *wane*) denoting deficiency, and *towen* trained, the p. part. of *teow*, to lead. *Wan* = prefix *un*. Early in the thirteenth century we find *untowen* for untrained ;—now *wanton*. **penal statutes**, laws made by Parliament, for the breach of which a penalty or punishment is enforced. **draw**, draw up, propose, prepare a draft of. **judge** is obj. case after behold (383), and **draw** is inf. mood = to draw. In 'The Vicar of Wakefield,' Goldsmith says : 'The work of eradicating crimes is not by making punishments familiar, but formidable.'

386 **Laws grind . . . rich men rule**. The government here is the same as in the line above. **wealth** in the following line is also obj. by behold, and **pillaged** is a passive participle qualifying wealth. Goldsmith writes in 'The Vicar of Wakefield,' ch. 19 : 'What they (the middle classes in the State) may then expect may be seen by turning our eyes to Holland, Genoa, or Venice, where *the laws govern the poor, and the rich govern the laws*.'

389 **Fear, pity, justice, indignation**, are noms. to start, tear, and bare.

390 **Tear off reserve,** i.e. give up concealment, be open and candid. **bare**. This word was originally merely an adjective, but has also taken the verbal meaning in the same way as *clean*, *light*, *black*, and other adjectives have done.

Till half a patriot, half a coward grown,
I fly from petty tyrants to the throne.

Yes, brother, curse with me that baleful hour
When first ambition struck at regal power;
And, thus polluting honour in its source,
Gave wealth to sway the mind with double force.

391–2 The order is: 'Till I, grown half a patriot, half a coward, fly,' &c. The meaning is: 'Till I, impelled by the mingled feelings of patriotism and fear of the evils threatening the land, appeal to the Sovereign to protect it against the injuries which petty tyrants inflict upon it.' **Coward** is said to be derived through the Fr. from the Lat. *cauda*, a tail, being one who 'turns tail' on his enemies. **tyrants.** A tyrant (Greek, τύραννος, Lat. *tyrannus*), formerly meant any despot or ruler who governed by his own arbitrary will, without senate or parliament. In this sense, the ancient sovereigns of Syracuse were called tyrants. Now, however, the term is applied to anyone who acts in a cruel and oppressive manner. **throne**, for the Sovereign who sits on the throne, by Metonymy. **petty**, Fr. *petit*, small. Cf. petticoat, pettifogger, pet (?) pettish (?)

393 **Brother.** cf. *to thee* (8). **baleful**, full of misery, sad, destructive, poisonous, from O. E. *bæl*, misery, mischief, poison. The noun *bale*, now gone out of use, was employed by Spenser.

> 'She look't about, and seeing one in mayle,
> Armèd to point, sought backe to turne againe;
> For light she hated as the deadly *bale*.'
>
> 'Faerie Queen,' i. 1, 16.

394 **Ambition** (346), **struck at**, attacked, aimed to destroy. The nobles have always been the greatest enemies to monarchical power. English History presents numerous instances of this.

395 **Honour in its source**, i.e. the kingly power.

'All degrees of nobility and honour are derived from the king, *as their fountain*.'—Blackstone, 'Commentaries.'

396 **Gave wealth**, i.e. gave to wealth the power to influence the mind with double force.

398 **Useless**, producing no good end. Observe the antithesis

Have we not seen, round Britain's peopled shore,
(Her useful sons exchanged for useless ore?)
Seen all her triumphs but destruction haste,
Like flaring tapers brightening as they waste?
Seen opulence, her grandeur to maintain,
Lead stern depopulation in her train,

between *useful sons* and *useless ore*. It is hard to say what the poet alludes to in this line, unless to emigration; but to this, the latter part of the line does not seem quite applicable. **Ore**, i.e. gold. Ore is properly metal in its impure state mixed with earthy matters, from which it is purified by smelting. In 'The Deserted Village' (269),

'Proud swells the tide with loads of freighted *ore*,'

the word stands for manufactured iron.

399 **Triumphs**, successes in war. **but**, only. The order is: 'Have we not seen all her triumphs haste (hasten, bring on rapidly) only destruction?'

400 **Like flaring tapers**, &c. i.e. like flickering candles, whose wax or tallow wastes away by reason of the unsteady flame, but which give out, in consequence, a brighter light.

401 **Opulence**, wealth. The order is: 'Have we not seen opulence, (in order) to maintain her grandeur, lead stern depopulation in her train?'

402 **Depopulation**, the act or process of unpeopling a place, depriving it of inhabitants. The Latin prefix *de* generally reverses the meaning of the word, or root to which it is attached. The Lat. words *populor*, and *depopulor*, both mean to lay waste, to unpeople a country. **train**. This word is derived from the Latin *traho*, to draw, through the French *traîner*. The *train* of a robe is that part of it which is *drawn* along the ground. A *train* of railway carriages is so called, because it is *drawn* along by the engine. A *train* of gunpowder, consists of gunpowder *drawn* out in a line, *Train* oil is so called, because *drawn* from the fat of whales. *Train*, in the text, means a long *drawn* line of followers or attendants. For the meaning of the passage, Cf.

'Trade's unfeeling *train*
Usurp the land, and dispossess the swain.'
'Deserted Village,' 63-64.

And over fields where scattered hamlets rose,
In barren solitary pomp repose?
Have we not seen, at pleasure's lordly call,
The smiling, long-frequented village fall?
Behold the duteous son, the sire decayed,
The modest matron, and the blushing maid,

The poet refers to what he considered the evils of emigration to America. Australia had been discovered, but was not colonised at this time. Laws have sometimes been passed to prevent emigration, but it has so many advantages, and in prosperous times, population increases so rapidly, and thus fills up the vacuum again, that these laws have soon been repealed.

403-4 Cf.

> 'Along the lawn, where scatter'd hamlets rose,
> Unwieldly wealth and cumbrous pomp repose.'
> 'Deserted Village,' 65-66.

hamlet, is derived from O. E. *ham*, an abode, and *let*, meaning little. So cir*clet*, a little circle; ring*let*, a little ring. *Ham* is seen in Bucking*ham*, Oak*ham*, &c. A hamlet is generally distinguished from a village by having no parish church, and is usually an outlying portion of a parish. **barren solitary pomp.** Cf.

> 'And desolation saddens all thy green:
> One only master grasps the whole domain,
> And half a village stints thy smiling plain.'
> 'Deserted Village,' 38-40.

405, &c. The poem of 'The Deserted Village' is the working out of the theme here introduced.

405 **Pleasure's lordly call,** the arbitrary will or pleasure of one man.

406 **Smiling,** prosperous, happy, **long-frequented,** i.e. well peopled for a long time. *Frequented* is derived from a Latin word *frequens*, meaning crowded, full of people.

407 **Sire** (313) **decayed,** worn out with years.

408 **Matron,** a mother, any married woman. Lat. *mater*, a mother; *matrona*, a married woman.

Forced from their homes, a melancholy train,
To traverse climes beyond the western main;
Where wild Oswego spreads her swamps around,
And Niagara stuns with thundering sound?
   E'en now, perhaps, as there some pilgrim strays
Through tangled forests and through dang'rous ways,

409 **Forced from their homes.** Cf.

> 'Downward they move, a melancholy band,
> Pass from the shore, and darken all the strand.'
> 'Deserted Village,' 401-2.

410 **Western main.** The Atlantic Ocean. The poet alludes to the emigration to America. Cf. (402). *Main* is an O.E. word, meaning power, strength; hence its applicability to the ocean. *Main* is also an adj. meaning principal, chief, strong, containing the chief part; and as applied to the sea may mean the *principal* sea, the ocean generally. So we have *main*guard, *main*spring, *main*mast, *main*sail, *main*stay, *main*land, i.e. the principal land, the continent generally.

411 **Oswego**, a river in the State of New York, North America, flowing into Lake Ontario, where the town of Oswego now stands. The river flows out of Lake Oneida, and the country around contains several smaller lakes, and is generally level. The marshy character of the district in Goldsmith's day justifies the use of the epithet **wild**, which, however, applies rather to the country than to the river. Cf. Wild Altama, 'Deserted Village' (344), where *wild* is used in the same sense.

412 **Niagara.** The river Niagara flows from Lake Erie to Lake Ontario, and is about thirty-six miles long. The Falls referred to by the poet occur about fourteen miles above the point where the river falls into the lake. Here the Niagara descends in two great falls separated from each other by a small island called Goats' Island. The fall on the American side is 162 feet high and 1,125 in width; that on the Canadian side is 149 feet high and 2,100 wide. The 'thundering sound' of the falls may sometimes be heard forty miles off. Niagara has, in this line, the accent on the third syllable. It should properly be on the second.

413 **Pilgrim** (197) traveller, **there**, in North America (413-418); with these lines compare 'The Deserted Village' (348-358).

Where beasts with man divided empire claim,
And the brown Indian marks with murderous aim;
There, while above the giddy tempest flies,
And all around distressful yells arise,
The pensive exile, bending with his wo,
* To stop too fearful, and too faint to go,
Casts a long look where England's glories shine,
And bids his bosom sympathize with mine.

415 **Divided empire claim**, i.e. dispute with each other supremacy over the land.

416 **Brown Indian.** The so-called Indians of North America are of a dark copper colour, and are often called 'red men.' The term Indian, however, is not correctly applied to others than natives of India. It was given to the natives of the American continent and islands by the first discoverers, who thought they had really reached India by sailing west; hence the name West Indies. **murderous aim.** They are very skilful marksmen.

417 **The giddy tempest**, the whirling tempest, a whirlwind. Cf.

> 'While oft in whirls the mad tornado flies.'
>
> 'Deserted Village,' 357.

418. **Distressful yells**, i.e. the yells of the 'brown Indians,' which fill the poor emigrant, 'the pensive exile,' with terror and distress. Yell is an *onomatopœia*, i.e. a word imitating the sound it expresses. Cf. rattle, clash, rumble.

419 **Pensive** (from the Lat. *pendo, pensum*, to weigh), conveys an idea of sadness as well as thoughtfulness.

> 'Anxious care the *pensive* nymph oppressed.' Pope

Milton, in 'Il Penseroso,' calls Melancholy '*pensive* Nun.' **Bending with his wo** (usually spelt woe), bending on account of it, i.e. with head bent down, as one in sad thought.

420 The order is: 'Too fearful to stop, and too faint to go on.' This beautiful line was written by Dr. Johnson when the poem was submitted to his friendly revision before publication. He at the same time added the last ten lines, with the exception of 435–6.

421 **Casts a long look**, i.e. mentally, of course. **England's glories.** Cf. lines 316–334.

Vain, very vain, my weary search to find
That bliss which only centres in the mind.
Why have I strayed from pleasure and repose,
To seek a good each government bestows?
In every government, though terrors reign,
Though tyrant kings or tyrant laws restrain,
* How small, of all that human hearts endure,
* That part which laws or kings can cause or cure!
* Still to ourselves in every place consigned,
* Our own felicity we make or find.

422 **Bosom sympathize with mine.** Sympathise is here in the inf. mood. The meaning is: 'He agrees with the opinion expressed in the concluding lines, viz., that man's happiness depends upon himself.'

423 Supply *is* after very vain.

424 **Which only centres,** &c., i.e. which is only to be found in the mind. Cf.

'Our hopes must *centre* in ourselves alone.' Dryden.

426 **A good** (26) **government,** a state, commonwealth or system of ruling. So we speak of the 'Government of Europe.'

427. **Terrors reign.** Had Goldsmith lived till the period of the great French Revolution in 1789, he would have seen such a Reign of Terror as he had never witnessed before. Supply *may* before reign.

428 The construction is: 'Though tyrant kings or tyrant laws *may* restrain.'

430 Supply *is* before *that part.* The poet means that the sufferings of the human heart are produced almost entirely by causes with which kings and laws have nothing to do, and cannot remedy; such, for instance, as ingratitude of children, sickness, bereavement, death, &c.

431-2 The order is: 'Still, we make or find our own felicity consigned (entrusted) to ourselves in every place.' Cf.

'The mind is its own place, and in itself,
Can make a heaven of hell, a hell of heaven.
Milton.

* With secret course, which no loud storms annoy,
* Glides the smooth current of domestic joy ;
The lifted axe, the agonising wheel,
Luke's iron crown, and Damiens' bed of steel,

433 The order is : 'The smooth current of domestic joy glides with secret course, which no loud storms annoy.'

434 **Smooth current**, destitute of excitement. **domestic joy**, i.e. the joy which a man makes or finds for himself in his home or family. Cf. 'Our own felicity' (432).

435 **Axe**, referring to the weapon with which traitors were formerly beheaded. **Agonizing wheel**, an allusion to a punishment called *breaking on the wheel*, which was formerly inflicted in France and other countries, and is still retained in Servia. The criminal was fastened to a cartwheel or to a frame in the form of a St. Andrew's cross X, and the executioner broke his legs with an iron bar. Sometimes the criminal's life was then mercifully taken by strangulation or by blows with the bar on the head and chest ; but too frequently he was left to expire with his legs doubled up under him. Cf.

'Who breaks a butterfly upon a wheel?' Pope.

436 **Luke's iron crown.** In 1513, two brothers, George and Luke Dosa (some say Zeck), placed themselves at the head of an insurrection of the peasantry in Hungary. Both were taken prisoners, and George, *not Luke*, in mockery of his supposed ambition to become king, was put to death by having a red-hot iron crown thrust down upon his head, and being compelled, at the same time, to sit on a red-hot iron throne. Whilst yet alive, his veins were opened, and his brother Luke was forced to drink the blood that flowed from them. Goldsmith has written Luke for George, either by mistake, or because it suited the line better. **Damiens' bed of steel.** In 1757, Robert Francis Damiens, a mad fanatic, attempted the assassination of Louis XV., King of France. He actually wounded the King slightly with a penknife as he was getting into his carriage. Damiens was put to the most exquisite tortures : his limbs were fastened with iron gyves to the scaffold ; his flesh was torn from his legs and body with hot pincers, boiling oil and molten lead were poured into his wounds ; then, being unable to stand, a bed was contrived, upon which he was kept alive

... courts to camps to cottage — [illegible]

2 ... Joshua Reynolds visiting [illegible]

be formed from teaching ... [illegible]

the ink of this line was still wet.

By sports like these are all their cares beguiled [illegible]

3 Schoolrooms — The poet speaks of the sea-breezes

as angels flying over the land ... means cool refre-

Pregnant quarry — The figure to be carved out

in the unhewn block of marble

Plethoric ill — diseased with superabundance of [illegible]

Stormy mansion — stormy country

Sanguine savage — any wild animal

Finer joy — joy in painting [illegible]

and carving

softer morals — cultivation of the fine arts,

politeness

[illegible]

21. Venice, Genoa, Turin, Florence

In the guilt of Venice ... [illegible]

On the ... Genoa ... Piedmont!

In the ... [illegible]

* To men remote from power but rarely known,
* Leave reason, faith, and conscience, all our own.

in torture for some time, and he was ultimately torn limb from limb by four horses. The 'bed of steel' probably refers to the 'rack,' to the torture of which Damiens was also subjected.

437 **To men remote,** &c., i.e. to those in private life and engaged neither in affairs of state nor in insurrections. **known** is a participle qualifying *axe, wheel, crown*, and *bed*, in the lines above, and these words are nominatives to *leave* in the line 438.

[illegible] [illegible] [illegible] [illegible]
modern English

[illegible] [illegible] the teaching practices
and methods of the period of the
fourteenth [illegible]
[illegible] [illegible] [illegible] [illegible]
[illegible] [illegible] [illegible]
[illegible] [illegible] [illegible]
[illegible] [illegible] [illegible]
[illegible] [illegible] [illegible] is connected
[illegible] 1358 and [illegible]
3 [illegible] [illegible] [illegible]
[illegible] [illegible] [illegible]
[illegible] [illegible] [illegible]
[illegible] [illegible]

NOTES.

NOTE A.

'Chamier,' said Johnson, 'once asked me what Goldsmith meant by *slow*, the last word in the first line of "The Traveller." Did he mean tardiness of locomotion?' Goldsmith, who would say something without consideration, answered 'Yes.' I was sitting by, and said, 'No, sir; you do not mean tardiness of locomotion. You mean that sluggishness of mind which comes upon a man in solitude.' Chamier believed I had written the line as much as if he had seen me write it. Boswell, 'Life of Dr. Johnson.' However, there is no doubt the poet did allude to *slowness of motion* induced by *heaviness of thought*. Mr. Forster, in his 'Life of Goldsmith,' says: 'The first point of the picture is *that*; the poet is moving slowly, his tardiness of gait measuring the heaviness of heart, the pensive spirit, the melancholy, of which it is the outward expression and sign.'

NOTE B.

One of Goldsmith's biographers says: 'He had a competent knowledge of French, knew a little Italian, and by means of these, and his acquaintance with Latin, he generally contrived to make himself understood in the several countries which he visited; but his great resource was his German flute. His knowledge was not indeed very scientific or extensive; what little he knew was principally by the ear; * yet, his performance, such as it was, generally procured him a ready welcome at the cottages where he sought a

* According to Sir John Hawkins, he did not even understand the character in which music is written.

night's hospitality, especially among the honest boors of Flanders, and the light-hearted peasantry of the South of France. When he approached a town, where his rude minstrelsy would have had to encounter severe critics, and a competition at once degrading and formidable, he abandoned his flute, and had recourse to his scholastic powers.'—Biography in 'Bohn's Edition.'

NOTE C.

The preamble of an act passed in 1799 (39 George III., c. 56), says: 'Whereas, before the passing of an act of the fifteenth of his present Majesty, many colliers, coal heavers, and salters *were bound for life to, and transferable with, the collieries and salt works where they worked*, but by the said act their bondage was taken off and they were declared to be free, notwithstanding which, many colliers and coal heavers and salters still continue in a state of bondage from not having complied with the provisions, or from having become subject to the penalties of that act,' &c. The act then declares them free from servitude.

ANNOTATED POEMS
OF
ENGLISH AUTHORS

EDITED BY THE

REV. E. T. STEVENS, M.A. OXON.

Joint-Editor of 'The Grade Lesson-Books' 'The Useful Knowledge Series' &c.

AND THE

REV. D. MORRIS, B.A. LOND.

Author of 'The Class-Book History of England' &c.

ELEGY IN A COUNTRY CHURCHYARD

BY THOMAS GRAY

ADAM MILLER AND COMPANY
11 WELLINGTON STREET WEST
TORONTO
1878

'The lowing herd winds slowly o'er the lea.'

ELEGY IN A COUNTRY CHURCHYARD.

---

1 THE curfew tolls the knell of parting day,
The lowing herd winds slowly o'er the lea,
The ploughman homeward plods his weary way,
And leaves the world to Darkness and to me.

1 **Curfew.** William I. introduced into this country, from Normandy, a law that all fires and lights should be extinguished on the ringing of a bell at eight o'clock in the evening. This was called the Curfew Bell, from the French *couvre feu*, to cover fire. It is still rung at Bristol and elsewhere, though the law is quite obsolete. **Knell,** the solemn note of a funeral bell. **'Parting,** i.e. departing. So, in Shakespeare's 'Merchant of Venice' we read, 'The quality of mercy is not '*strain'd*,' for restrained. Many other similar abbreviations occur throughout his plays, as—'cause,

2 Now fades the glimmering landscape on the sight,
  And all the air a solemn stillness holds,
Save where the beetle wheels his droning flight,
  And drowsy tinklings lull the distant folds;

3 Save that, from yonder ivy-mantled tow'r,
  The moping owl does to the Moon complain
Of such as, wand'ring near her secret bow'r,
  Molest her ancient, solitary reign.

for because; 'friend, for befriend; 'longing, for belonging; 'stroy'd, for destroyed, &c. **Lea**, a meadow, field, &c.:—an old English word found in various forms—*lay*, *ley*, *leigh*, &c.—and still existing in the names of numerous towns and villages; as *Lay*ham, Hor*ley*, *Leigh*ton, Had*leigh*, *Leigh*.

2 **Glimmering**. To glimmer, frequentative of gleam, is to shine faintly or at intervals. This expression is used of the landscape because it is only dimly visible just after sunset. **Landscape**, formerly written 'landskip,' meant originally a painted picture of the view over a tract of country, rather than the thing itself. The termination is probably the same as *ship*, meaning the form or character of a thing, as in friend*ship*, lord*ship*, hard*ship*. **Save**, a verb used as a preposition, like 'except,' which is properly an abbreviation of the participle *excepted*. **Beetle**, the May-bug, door-beetle, or cockchafer, which flies about on summer evenings, is here alluded to. The grub of this insect remains in the ground three complete years before coming to its perfect state, and is so voracious that it does great injury to the roots of grass and trees, &c. **Droning flight**. A drone is a bee that does not collect honey; hence the term droning means buzzing about in a useless manner. **Drowsy tinklings**, i.e., of the sheep-bells. The oldest male sheep of a flock has usually a bell fastened with a strap round his neck; hence he is called the bell-wether, and the rest of the sheep follow the sound, thus keeping together. The tinklings are called 'drowsy' because of their slow, dull, and monotonous sound.

3 **Ivy-mantled**, i.e. covered with ivy as with a mantle or cloak. **Moping owl**. To mope is to be out of spirits or dull. **To the Moon complain**. The owl flies abroad in search of its prey at night, and its eyes are so constructed that it can see

4 Beneath those rugged elms, that yew-tree's shade,
Where heaves the turf in many a mould'ring heap,
Each in his narrow cell for ever laid,
The rude forefathers of the hamlet sleep.

5 The breezy call of incense-breathing Morn,
The swallow, twitt'ring from the straw-built shed,
The cock's shrill clarion, or the echoing horn,
No more shall rouse them from their lowly bed.

6 For them no more the blazing hearth shall burn,
Or busy housewife ply her evening care;
No children run to lisp their sire's return;
Or climb his knees the envied kiss to share.

better at dusk than in the full light of day; it therefore chooses dark places to live in. The poet represents the owl as complaining to the moon when passers-by disturb her, and perhaps frighten away the mice, &c., on which she feeds.

4 **Heaves.** To heave is to lift up, to raise, as 'to heave the anchor' on board ship; and hence Heaven is a place heaved or lifted up. Sometimes heaves is used as an intransitive verb, to rise, and is so used in this passage. **Narrow cell,** i.e. the grave. **Rude forefathers.** Rude is from the Latin *rudis*, and means simply rough, uncultivated, not polished in manners. **Hamlet.** '*Ham*' is an old English word, meaning an abode, and still exists in *Ham*, Oak*ham*, Bucking*ham*, &c.; '*let*' is a diminutive suffix, meaning *little*, as in stream*let*, rivu*let*, circ*let*.

5 **Incense-breathing Morn,** i.e. filled with sweet perfumes of flowers. Incense is properly a kind of gum which, when burnt, emits a fragrant odour. **Cock's shrill clarion.** There is a poem of the Middle Ages, very popular at that time, called 'Reynard the Fox.' Various animals are introduced in it under peculiar names, which, owing to the old popularity of the poem, still adhere to them; thus, the fox is called Reynard, the bear Bruin, and the cock Chanticleer (which name the poet originally inserted here, but afterwards altered) on account of his shrill crowing. The clarion is a kind of trumpet which gives a clearer, shriller sound than the common one. The word is derived, through the French, from the Latin *clarus*, clear, shrill. **Horn,** i.e. of the hunter.

6 **Housewife,** sometimes written 'huswife,' and contracted

7 Oft did the harvest to their sickle yield;
Their furrow oft the stubborn glebe has broke;
How jocund did they drive their team afield!
How bow'd the woods beneath their sturdy stroke!

8 Let not Ambition mock their useful toil,
Their homely joys, and destiny obscure;
Nor Grandeur hear with a disdainful smile
The short and simple annals of the poor.

into 'hussif,' meaning a case for needles and thread; and 'hussy,' or 'huzzy,' a wench, woman, now used in an uncomplimentary sense, though originally not so. **Evening care**, i.e. needlework, or other employment. **Sire**, the old French word for a knight or lord. It commonly means father with us, and is always used as a title of respect, especially in addressing a king. Our common word Sir is an abbreviation of Sire.

7 **Stubborn**, i.e. hard to be turned up with the plough. A stub is a short, thick stock of a tree or other plant, left when the rest is cut off, and is the same word as stump. Stubble is derived from this word, the *le* being what is called a frequentative termination, and denoting that a great number of stubs are met with in stubble. Stubborn means like a stub, i.e. stiff, unbending, obstinate. **Glebe** (Lat. *gleba*) is properly any turf, soil, or land; but is employed now to signify that which belongs to the incumbent, as such, of a church. **Jocund** (Lat. *jucundus*), joyful, merry—adjective used for adverb, which is common in poetry. **Afield**, i.e. to or on the field. The Old English prefix *a*, meaning to, at, or on, is also seen in *a*bed, *a*board, *a*shore, *a*jar (so said of a door which is in such a position that a slight movement, a jar, will close it). **Sturdy**, hardy, stout, strong, stiff.

8 **Ambition**, a desire of honour or power, from the Latin *ambi*, about, and *eo*, *itum*, to go. The word meant originally among the Romans a going up and down the city asking for votes. Those who did this were clad in white, or distinguished by some white article of dress, and were hence called 'candidati' (Lat. *candidus*, white), from which our word candidate is derived. **Annals**, from Latin *annus*, a year, are yearly records of events.

9 The boast of Heraldry, the pomp of Pow'r,
And all that Beauty, all that Wealth e'er gave,
Await, alike, th' inevitable hour;
The paths of Glory lead but to the grave.

10 Nor you, ye proud, impute to these the fault,
If Mem'ry o'er their tomb no trophies raise,
Where, thro' the long-drawn aisle and fretted vault,
The pealing anthem swells the note of praise.

11 Can storied urn, or animated bust,
Back to its mansion call the fleeting breath?
Can Honour's voice provoke the silent dust,
Or Flatt'ry soothe the dull cold ear of death?

9 **Heraldry.** The science which treats of coats-of-arms and crests. **Inevitable hour,** the hour that cannot be avoided, i.e. the hour of death. **Paths of Glory,** i.e. all human glory, whether of literature, or arms, or anything else, ends at last in death.

10 **Trophies,** things preserved as memorials of a victory, such as arms and standards taken from the enemy. These, or their own arms, were frequently placed over the tombs of warriors, as may be seen in Canterbury Cathedral, Westminster Abbey, &c. **Long-drawn aisle,** i.e. the long aisle of a cathedral or other large church, alluding particularly to those of what is commonly called Gothic, but is more properly known as Early English, architecture. **Fretted vault,** i.e. a stone roof ornamented with fretwork. Fret is from an old French word (*fréter*), signifying the interlacing of bars. Frets in heraldry are bars crossing and interlacing each other. So a fretted roof is one ornamented with bands or fillets crossing each other in different patterns. Fret, to grieve, is another word entirely, being derived from the old English *fretan*, to eat away, as 'a moth fretteth a garment.' The allusion here is to costly tombs of kings and nobles in abbeys and cathedral churches, such as those of Westminster, Canterbury, &c.

11 **Storied urn.** The ancient Greeks and Romans used to burn their dead and place their ashes in urns made for the purpose. These urns were frequently ornamented outside with pictures illustrating the story or history of the deceased person. Such an urn as this the poet calls a storied urn. Windows of churches are often

12 Perhaps in this neglected spot is laid
  Some heart once pregnant with celestial fire ;
Hands that the rod of Empire might have sway'd,
  Or wak'd to extasy the living Lyre.

similarly painted with histories taken from Holy Scripture. Milton, in 'Il Penseroso,' describes these as—

'*Storied* windows richly dight,
Casting a dim religious light.'

Animated, i.e. looking as lifelike as possible. **Bust,** from Ital. *busto*, meant originally the body of a man, the trunk without arms or legs; then a statue representing the head and upper part of the trunk. *Busk*, which appears to be the same word somewhat modified, was used in the North of France to represent the same thing. Bust and busk were then used to indicate a garment closely fitting the body, and the latter word is still used to signify a piece of whalebone or steel employed to stiffen the bodice of a lady's dress. **Mansion** (Lat. maneo, *to stay*, mansio, *an abiding-place*), a house, home, abode, generally used of a large house. The human body is here alluded to as the mansion or abode of the breath of life. **Provoke** (Lat. pro, *forth*, voco, *to call*), to summon forth to life again.

12 **This neglected spot,** the churchyard of Stoke Pogis, in Buckinghamshire, though the poem is said to have been actually written at Grantchester. Neglected here probably means simply not known to the public, unnoticed. **Pregnant,** Lat. *prægnans*, filled with, teeming with. **Celestial fire,** the gift of poetry, which was supposed to be sent from heaven by the gods; or it may mean talent generally. In the old mythology Prometheus is said to have made the figure of a man with clay, and to have animated it with fire, which, with the assistance of Minerva, he brought down from heaven. As a punishment for this, Jupiter chained him to Mount Caucasus, with a vulture perpetually gnawing his liver. **The rod of Empire,** i.e. the sceptre as an emblem of sovereignty. **Extasy,** sometimes written ecstasy, is from a Greek word ἔκστασις (ekstasis), which means the removal of a thing from its proper place; hence distraction of the mind from terror, astonishment, or joy. **Living Lyre,** any musical instrument of the nature of a harp. By living Lyre is probably meant one which gives forth peculiarly sweet sounds under the hands of a skilful performer.

13 But Knowledge to their eyes her ample page
Rich with the spoils of Time did ne'er unroll;
Chill Penury repress'd their noble rage,
And froze the genial current of the soul.

14 Full many a gem, of purest ray serene,
The dark unfathom'd caves of ocean bear;
Full many a flow'r is born to blush unseen,
And waste its sweetness on the desert air.

13 **Knowledge,** an example of Personification. **Ample** (Lat. *amplus*, large), referring to the large number of subjects with which Knowledge has to do. **Spoils of Time.** Spoils (Lat. *spolia*) are things taken from an enemy in war. By the spoils of Time are meant the various kinds of Knowledge that time and study have enabled men to win from Ignorance. These have been preserved in books, but knowledge could not unroll her ample page to the persons alluded to by the poet because of their ignorance and poverty. **Penury** (Lat. *penuria*), poverty; another example of Personification. This word formerly included the idea of meanness and niggardliness, which is still retained in penurious and penuriousness. Bishop Jeremy Taylor, who lived from 1613 to 1667, writes, 'God sometimes punishes one sin with another; pride with adultery; drunkenness with murder; *penury* with oppression;' as in the case of the Jews in England in the reign of King John. **Repress'd their noble rage,** i.e. those of them who had noble desires of distinguishing themselves were kept down by poverty. **Froze the genial current,** i.e. checked their desires, just as frost checks the current of a stream by freezing it.

14 **Many a gem.*** A gem is a precious stone (Lat. *gemma*). The expression *many a* is an abbreviation for *many of.* Originally it would have stood *many of gems*; many being a noun. This expression became shortened into *many o' gems*, just as we say what's o' clock? for what's of the clock? In the course of time this *o'* came to be written *a*, as it was pronounced; and at last, the origin of the *a* being forgotten, people thought it incorrect to say *many a gems*, and consequently said *many a gem.* **Of purest ray,** i.e. perfect in colour. **Serene** (Lat. *serenus*), clear. **Bear,** i.e. have,

* Archbishop Trench thus explains it in *English Past and Present.* See Note A at the end.

15 Some village-Hampden, that with dauntless breast
The little tyrant of his fields withstood;
Some mute inglorious Milton here may rest;
Some Cromwell, guiltless of his country's blood.

contain. **Unfathom'd,** a fathom is a measure of six feet, used only in measuring depths. Unfathomed is that which cannot be, or has not been, measured. At a great depth the water of the sea is so dense that even lead sinks with great difficulty. **Many a flow'r,** cf. 'many a gem' above. **Waste its sweetness,** i.e. its perfume, as the violet. **Desert air,** not the air of a desert, but of any deserted or lonely place where it is unobserved by man.

15 **Some village-Hampden.** John Hampden was a leader of the Parliamentarian forces against those of Charles I., when he attempted to levy taxes without the authority of the House of Commons. He was slain in the battle of Chalgrove Field, Oxfordshire. **Tyrant of his fields.** A tyrant now is a person who acts in a cruel and oppressive manner. Formerly, however, a tyrant (Greek τύραννος, Lat. *tyrannus*) meant any despot, or arbitrary ruler. In the poem the village-Hampden is represented as withstanding what he considered oppression, on the part of his richer or more powerful neighbours, in the same fearless spirit as John Hampden withstood Charles I. **Mute,** dumb, not able to speak, i.e. one who did not write poetry, as Milton did; not, perhaps, because he lacked natural talent, but because he had not the opportunity of having it cultivated and brought to light. **Inglorious,** not renowned, not famous; though sometimes this word has a stronger meaning, the very opposite of glorious, as *an inglorious retreat*, i.e. a disgraceful one. **Milton.** John Milton, the author of 'Paradise Lost,' 'Paradise Regained,' 'L'Allegro,' 'Il Penseroso,' 'Comus,' &c., was born in London, in 1608, and died 1674. He was the greatest epic poet the world has ever seen. The poet means that possibly some one of the persons whose remains lie in the 'neglected spot' might have become as famous as Milton if he had had the same advantages of education. **Some Cromwell.** Oliver Cromwell was a country gentleman who became member of Parliament for Huntingdon, and afterwards the leader of the Parliamentarian forces against those of Charles I., on the execution of whom he was made Lord-Protector of the Commonwealth of England. He died in 1658. The poet here takes the Royalist view.

16 Th' applause of list'ning senates to command,
The threats of pain and ruin to despise,
To scatter plenty o'er a smiling land,
And read their hist'ry in a nation's eyes,

17 Their lot forbade: nor circumscrib'd alone
Their growing virtues, but their crimes confin'd;
Forbade to wade through slaughter to a throne,
And shut the gates of Mercy on mankind;

16 **List'ning senates,** i.e. Houses of Parliament listening to some famous orator. Their lot forbade them, i.e. prevented them from becoming orators and members of Parliament, and, therefore, from commanding the applause of listening senates. **Threats of pain and ruin to despise,** their humble position did not expose them to the threats of pain and ruin to which prominent persons are exposed in troublous times, but who, as history shows, have often despised them. **To scatter plenty,** i.e. to be the means of causing great national prosperity. **To read their history,** &c. probably means to become what are commonly called public characters, whose history everyone knows, and who read the success of their efforts for the good of their fellow-countrymen in the sentiments which the latter entertain towards them.

17 **Their lot forbade,** i.e. prevented their doing the things mentioned in the preceding verse. **Circumscrib'd** (Lat. *circum*, around, *scribo*, to write), surrounded, limited, confined, narrowed. **Crimes confin'd**; as they had not the opportunity of becoming eminent on account of good and noble deeds, so they had not the opportunity of becoming notorious on account of wicked and cruel ones. **Forbade,** i.e. their lot, their humble position, combined with their want of education and opportunity, forbade, &c. **To wade through slaughter to a throne**; to become king through the defeat of an enemy in battle, as William I. had done at Hastings; or by murder, as Henry IV. had done by the murder of Richard II., and as Richard III. had done by that of his nephews, Edward V. and Richard Duke of York. **To shut the gates of mercy,** i.e. to allow no mercy to be shown, to act in a cruel and unmerciful manner.

18 The struggling pangs of conscious Truth to hide,
To quench the blushes of ingenuous Shame,
Or heap the shrine of Luxury and Pride
With incense kindled at the Muse's flame.

19 Far from the madding crowd's ignoble strife
Their sober wishes never learn'd to stray;
Along the cool, sequester'd vale of life
They kept the noiseless tenor of their way.

18 **Pangs of conscious Truth to hide.** Their lot forbade them to conceal what they thought the truth through fear of persecution, because they occupied so humble a position that no one would have paid any heed to them, and consequently, they had no need to quench the blushes of ingenuous shame, as those did who pretended, in order to avoid persecution, to believe doctrines which 'conscious truth' told them were false. **Shrine** (O.E. *scrin*), a case in which something sacred is deposited. This was frequently made of stone, handsomely carved, and contained the remains of some person eminent for piety and valour. Pilgrims formerly visited these shrines in great numbers, and deposited on them valuable offerings of gold, jewellery, &c. The shrine of Thomas a' Becket in Canterbury Cathedral was thus adorned with gold and jewels to the value of many thousands of pounds. **Luxury and Pride,** examples of Personification. **Incense** was frequently burnt before shrines; the word is here used for *flattery*. **Muse's flame.** The ancient poets personified the various intellectual exercises of mankind under the name of Muses. These were said to be the daughters of Jove and Mnemosyne, i.e. Memory. Some say there were three Muses, Memory, Song, and Meditation. Others say there were nine, viz. History, Tragedy, Comedy, Use of the Flute, The Lyre, The Lute, Heroic Verse, Astrology, and Rhetoric. The poet here alludes to those who debased the art of poetry by writing, in hope of reward, flattering verse in praise of persons who were addicted to habits of luxury and pride.

19 **Madding,** not *maddening*, which means making mad, but simply excited, furious, raging, alluding to the strife of competition for wealth and power so frequently met with in populous cities. **Ignoble** (Lat. in, *not*, nobilis, *noble*) not noble, worthless. **Sober** (Lat. *sobrius*), temperate, calm, regular, moderate. **Se-**

20 Yet ev'n these bones from insult to protect,
Some frail memorial still erected nigh,
With uncouth rhymes and shapeless sculpture deck'd,
Implores the passing tribute of a sigh.

21 Their name, their years, spelt by th' unletter'd Muse,
The place of fame and elegy supply;
And many a holy text around she strews,
That teach the rustic moralist to die.

quester'd, adj., retired. Sequester, as a verb, means to take possession of property for the benefit of creditors, to separate it from its owner for a time, and hence to separate oneself from other people, withdraw, retire. It is derived from the Latin *sequester*, a mediator, a go-between or agent in cases of bribery, and so a person into whose hands money or any other matter of dispute was placed until the question was decided. **Tenor,** continued course (Lat. *teneo*, to hold), **of their way,** their mode of life, removed from the bustle of the world.

20 **Frail memorial,** probably the wooden tablet on which the name, &c. of the deceased was painted, such as is now frequently seen in country churchyards; said to be frail because not so strong or lasting as gravestones. **Uncouth** (O. E. *uncuth*, from *cunnan*, to know) now means odd, strange, unusual, awkward, but formerly simply unknown. So *barbarous*, which at first meant only foreign, came to mean savage and wild. So *outlandish*, which in old English meant simply not belonging to the land or country, i.e. foreign, came to mean strange and awkward. The change in meaning arises from the disposition of mankind to dislike everything with which they are unacquainted. One old writer (Puttenham, in the 'Art of English Poesy') says the Greek and Latin languages are *uncouth* to the common people. And Milton says in 'L'Allegro,'—

'Find out some *uncouth* cell
Where brooding darkness spreads his jealous wings.'

Shapeless sculpture, figures of angels, &c., roughly carved in the stone or wood. **Implores the passing tribute,** alluding to the verses on tombstones which often call upon the passer-by to stop and moralise on death, and sympathise with the bereaved.

21 **Unletter'd Muse,** unlearned, alluding to the writer of the

22 For who, to dumb Forgetfulness a prey,
This pleasing, anxious being e'er resign'd,
Left the warm precincts of the cheerful day,
Nor cast one longing, ling'ring look behind?

23 On some fond breast the 'parting soul relies,
Some pious drops the closing eye requires:
Ev'n from the tomb the voice of Nature cries,
Ev'n in our ashes live their wonted fires.

'uncouth rhymes' mentioned above. **Elegy** (Greek ἐλεγεῖον, *elegion*), a mournful kind of poem, a funeral song. **She**, i.e. the Muse (see v. 18). **Rustic**, from Lat. rus, *the country*; rusticus, *belonging to the country*. **Moralist**, the person who stops to read the holy texts and moralise on them. **To die**, i.e. how to die.

22 **To dumb Forgetfulness a prey.** Forgetfulness is here personified as a wild beast preying upon people. The poet means that no one under ordinary circumstances has ever died in such a state of forgetfulness as not to look back with some longing upon the days that are past. **Longing, ling'ring look.** The young student will here notice the pleasing effect of these three words coming together, and all beginning with the same letter. This is called Alliteration, and was the prominent feature of Old English poetry. There are several other more or less perfect examples of it in this poem:—

v. 1. The ploughman homeward plods his weary way.
v. 5. The cock's shrill clarion, or the echoing horn.
v. 15. Some mute inglorious Milton here may rest.
v. 26. And pore upon the brook that babbles by.
v. 27. Or craz'd with care, or cross'd in hopeless love.

Other pleasing examples of Alliteration in this beautiful poem the young student will readily discover.

23 **Fond breast,** i.e. affectionate, loving; but *fond* formerly meant foolish, silly; and a *fondling* was a foolish person. Bishop Barrow, in one of his sermons, describes a profane swearer as a *fondling*. The XXII. Article of the Church of England says the Romish doctrine concerning Purgatory, pardons, &c. is a *fond* thing vainly invented. **'Parting,** i.e. departing (see v. 1). **Relies,**

24 For thee, who, mindful of th' unhonour'd dead,
Dost in these lines their artless tale relate,
If, 'chance, by lonely Contemplation led,
Some kindred spirit shall enquire thy fate ;

25 Haply, some hoary-headed swain may say,
'Oft have we seen him, at the peep of dawn,
'Brushing, with hasty steps, the dews away,
'To meet the Sun upon the upland lawn.

leans, rests. **Pious drops**, i.e. tears, which, the poet says, the dying person desires to be shed for him. **Ashes**, remains, in allusion to the ancient custom of cremation or burning the bodies of the dead. **Wonted**, accustomed. **Fires**, i.e. the higher desires and aspirations of men. The poet says that these live, even when those who conceived them are dead, and are often expressed on their tombstones or otherwise remembered.

24 **For thee.** The poet here alludes to himself. **Mindful,** bearing them in mind, thinking of them. **Unhonour'd**, not honoured, i.e. having no honour bestowed upon them ; *dishonoured* is a much stronger word, meaning disgraced. **Artless tale**, i.e. simple history. **'Chance**, for perchance, perhaps (see 'parting, v. 1.) **Contemplation**, an example of Personification. **Kindred**, of like kind or nature, from O. E. *kin*, which means relationship. In this sense the word kindred, as a noun, is now generally used. So *kindly* formerly meant according to nature, natural. In the Litany we pray that God will be pleased 'to give and preserve to our use the *kindly* fruits of the earth.' So Sir Thomas More, in his 'Life of Richard III.,' says that Richard thought by murdering his two nephews in the Tower of London to make himself a *kindly* king, i.e. one of the same family, being their father's brother. Shakespeare makes Hamlet say, when speaking of his uncle who had married his mother after murdering his father, he was 'a little more than *kin* and less than *kind*.'

25 **Haply**, perhaps. **Hoary** (O. E. har, *white*), hoar frost is white frost, sometimes called ryme. Hoary-headed, i.e. gray-headed, white with age. **Swain** (O. E. swān), a countryman. **To meet the Sun**, i.e. to see him rise. **Upland**, sloping upwards. **Lawn**, or laund, a meadow formerly, now a plot of grass in front of a house.

26 'There, at the foot of yonder nodding beech,
'That wreathes its old fantastic roots so high,
'His listless length at noontide would he stretch,
'And pore upon the brook that babbles by.

27 'Hard by yon wood, now smiling, as in scorn,
'Mutt'ring his wayward fancies, he would rove;
'Now drooping, woeful wan, like one forlorn,
'Or craz'd with care, or cross'd in hopeless love.

'Russet *lawns* and fallows gray,
Where the nibbling flocks do stray.'—Milton, '*L'Allegro.*'

The author is here describing his own habits.

26 **Nodding beech,** waving in the breeze. **Wreathe,** to twist. **Fantastic roots,** alluding to the curious forms into which they are often twisted. **Listless length**; *listen, listless, listful,* are all derived from an O. E. word, hlystan, *to hearken, give ear to*; hence, *attend to, be attentive.* Listless, therefore, means inattentive, idle; whilst listful, which is now obsolete, meant the reverse. The poet speaks of himself as lying at full length on the grass at the foot of a shady beech, with nothing else to do but to 'pore upon the brook that babbles by.' **Pore,** to look with continued attention or application; hence *poreblind,* now written *purblind,* means shortsighted, i.e. unable to see a thing distinctly without looking very closely and attentively at it. **Babble.** This word belongs to a class called onomatopœic (from the Greek ὄνομα, onoma, *a name*; and ποιέω, poieo, *to make*); viz. those which imitate the sounds they represent. Many of these are common to several languages. Familiar examples in English are: bray, bleat, rattle, clash, smash, rumble, murmur.

27 **Hard by,** very near. **Smiling, muttering, drooping, woeful, wan, craz'd, cross'd.** These words describe the varying mood of the poet. **Wan,** faded, pale, from an O. E. word *wanian,* to decrease, decline; whence wane, to fade. Wan had formerly many compounds which are now become obsolete, viz.:—wanhope = waned-hope, despair; wanluck = waned-luck, misfortune; wanthrift = waned-thrift, extravagance; wanwit = waned-wit, folly; wangrace = waned-grace, wickedness; wantrust = waned-trust, distrust.

28 'One morn I miss'd him on the 'custom'd hill,
'Along the heath, and near his fav'rite tree:
'Another came; nor yet beside the rill,
'Nor up the lawn, nor at the wood was he.

29 'The next, with dirges due, in sad array,
'Slow through the churchway path we saw him borne.
'Approach and read (for thou canst read) the lay,
''Graved on the stone beneath yon aged thorn.'

THE EPITAPH.

30 Here rests his head upon the lap of Earth,
A youth to Fortune and to Fame unknown;
Fair Science frown'd not on his humble birth,
And Melancholy mark'd him for her own.

28 **'Custom'd,** for accustomed (cf. 'parting, v. 1). **Nor . . . nor,** for neither . . . nor. The old use was *ne . . . ne*, which at length developed into *nor . . . nor* and then, *neither . . . nor*.

29 **Dirges.** A dirge is a funeral song. In O. E. the word is always spelt *dirige*, which is the present imperative second person singular of the Latin verb *dirigo*, to direct, to guide, and was probably the first word in a Latin psalm or prayer formerly used at funerals. The modern spelling came into use in the seventeenth century. Wickliffe enumerates among the services of the Church, 'Matins, Mass, Evensong, and Placebo, and *Dirige*.' **Slow,** adj. for adv. slowly. Poets often use adjectives instead of adverbs for the sake of the metre, but it is not allowable in prose. **Lay,** O. E. *ley*, a song or poem. **'Grav'd,** for engraved (see 'parting, v. 1), from O. E. *grafan*, to dig, to carve. Hence a grave is a place dug out. An engraver in wood, metal, or stone digs out the material in which he works with a graving-tool. *Grave*, in the sense of serious, important, is a quite different word, being derived from the Latin *gravis*, heavy, important, severe.

30 **Epitaph,** an inscription on a tomb, from the Greek ἐπί (epi), *upon*, and τάφος (taphos), *a tomb*. **Lap of Earth.** The poet here speaks of the Earth as his mother, in allusion to the Scriptural

31 Large was his bounty, and his soul sincere,
Heav'n did a recompense as largely send:
He gave to Mis'ry all he had—a tear;
He gain'd from Heav'n ('twas all he wish'd)—a friend.

32 No farther seek his merits to disclose,
Or draw his frailties from their dread abode
(There they alike in trembling hope repose),
The bosom of his Father and his God.

account of the Creation of Man from the 'dust of the ground,' and represents himself as sleeping the sleep of death with his head resting upon her lap, after the manner of a little child. **Humble birth.** The poet's mother, who was separated from her husband on account of his cruelty, gained her living as a milliner. **Fortune, Fame, Science, Melancholy.** These are all Personified. Melancholy is derived from the Greek μέλας (melas), *black*, and χολή (chole), *bile*, because the old physicians thought that a particular kind of moody madness which they called by this name was caused by too much black bile in the blood. Now, however, the word is used to indicate merely a heavy, and more or less permanent, sadness. **Marked him for her own,** in allusion to the custom of marking cattle, &c. with the name or initials of their owner. The poet here means that he was of a melancholy disposition.

31 **Bounty** (Fr. *bonté*), charity, liberality. It was large, because he gave all he had, i.e. a tear. **Sincere,** honest, upright, true; but originally unmixed, unadulterated, pure. It is said by some to be derived from Lat. *sine*, without, and *cera*, wax, in allusion to honey from which all the wax has been carefully removed.

32 **Frailties,** weaknesses, sins. The dread abode of these frailties is the bosom of God, meaning that the poet has confessed them all to Him. **Alike,** i.e. both his merits and his frailties now rest in the bosom of God.

NOTE A.

Many a. The indefinite numeral adjective *many* is the Old Eng. *maneg*, Gothic *manegs*, and is akin to the same root *mah*, from which *more* comes. The indefinite article *a* was developed after the Norman Conquest from the Old English numeral *one* (ân).

The use of *a* after *many* is first seen in 'The Brut' of Layamon, a Worcestershire monk about the date A.D. 1200. He has 'on moni are wisen' (many are wise) and 'mony enne thing' (many a thing). About a century later, in a Midland poem called 'The Harrowing of Hell,' we find the following:

'I shal go fro man to man,
And reve þe of *mani an*'—(one).

The last two words are met with in other works of the same period, and, in a few years afterwards, Robert Manning's 'Northern Psalter' has *many one*. Spenser in the 'Faerie Queene' has the same phrase, and also 'many a man.' Shakespeare occasionally puts the article before 'many,' as 'a many thousand French,' and we still retain this use with *great* between, as 'a great many persons.'

The phrase *many a* is to be explained as a large number taken distributively—each one of many.

'Many,' like other adjectives, is sometimes used as a noun, as by Shakespeare:

'A *many* of our bodies,' *Hen. V.* v. 3.

'O thou fond *many*,' *Second Part of Hen. IV.* i. 3.

'The rank-scented *many*,' }
'In *many's* looks,' } *Sonnets*, 93.

'A *meanye* of us were called together,' Latimer's *Sermons*.

Archbishop Trench in 'English Past and Present' (4th ed. pp. 161, 162) explains the use of *many a* on the supposition that *many* was originally the old French noun *mesnee*, *maisnee*; Low Lat. *maisnada*, a family: from Latin *minores natu*, younger sons, dependants, menials. This noun, in its original sense of 'a household, a retinue,' occurs in a sacred poem A.D. 1320 called 'Cursor Mundi;' and in an allusion to the 'Visit of the Wise Men and Flight into Egypt,' we read:—

'Son was Joseph ready bun,
Wit naghtertale he went o tun,
Wit Maria mild and fair *meiné*.'

About a score years later, in a translation of St. Matthew's Gospel (ch. xxiv.) by a monk, Dan Michel of Northgate, Kent, we have in v. 25:

'to huam be-longeþ (th) moche *mayné*.'

Our Version has 'whom his lord hath made ruler over his household.'

In 'William and the Werwolf,' a Salopian composition of about the year 1340, quoted in Morris's 'Specimens of Early English,' p. 243, we have

'Wiþ alle his menskful meyné, that moche was and nobul.'

It is manifest that this noun is not the *mony* of Layamon and later writers. The old French word soon passed away, and the examples of its use show that it had no other meaning than a 'retinue or household.'

www.ingramcontent.com/pod-product-compliance
Lightning Source LLC
Chambersburg PA
CBHW022351020726
47500CB00002B/222

* 9 7 8 3 3 3 7 2 1 2 3 2 2 *